W9-COB-068

# *A*
# *CANDLE*
# *IN*
# *HER ROOM*

RUTH M. ARTHUR

# *A*
# CANDLE
# IN
# HER ROOM

*Illustrations by Margery Gill*

AN ALADDIN BOOK
*Atheneum*

PUBLISHED BY ATHENEUM
COPYRIGHT © 1966 BY RUTH M. ARTHUR
ALL RIGHTS RESERVED
PUBLISHED SIMULTANEOUSLY IN CANADA BY
MCCLELLAND & STEWART LTD.
MANUFACTURED IN THE UNITED STATES OF AMERICA BY
CONNECTICUT PRINTERS, INC., BLOOMFIELD, CONN.
FIRST ALADDIN EDITION

*For the Curtis family,*
*and all my friends in Pembrokeshire*

# CONTENTS

PART I  *MELISSA*

# CHAPTER ONE

I SUPPOSE IF WE HAD NOT COME TO LIVE IN PEMBROKE-shire, Judith, Briony and I, this story would never have been written, for in another set of circumstances our lives might have run very differently. There would have been no Dido.

I am Melissa, the eldest of the three Mansell girls and until I was twelve we had always lived in a shabby house in a nondescript street in a dull part of London.

Our father was a doctor—a good doctor too— but we never had any money, for he often neglected to send bills to his patients who were mostly poorer than our-selves. Those were the days long before the National

Health Service, and in poor districts many doctors found it hard to make ends meet.

Our mother did all the cooking, and made our clothes, as well as taking a kindly interest in our neighbors and in our father's patients. She was helped in the house by a little sixteen-year-old maid, Emily, who insisted on writing her name "Emmy Lee"; she was devoted to all of us.

We sisters attended a prim little day school run for the daughters of impoverished professional men, and I often felt sorry for Briony because she had to wear my old dresses at school. They were always patched at the elbows and had to be taken in and up at various places, for Briony was three years younger than I.

Judith who came in between us was almost as tall as I was, and of a dazzling fairness, while Briony and I were dark. The colors that suited her were different from ours and, perhaps because of a certain natural elegance, Judith's clothes, whether handed down from an older cousin or from my mother, looked as if they had been specially made for her alone—she wore them with an air.

Suddenly, as if at the wave of a magic wand, all this was changed.

Our father's old Aunt Lucia died at Newcove in Pembrokeshire, leaving her money and her beautiful old house to us, on condition that we went to live there.

Our father was jubilant, for many of his boyhood holidays had been spent on that enchanting coast. Our mother, who loved the country, rejoiced at returning to it and to a less harassed life, which Aunt Lucia's money would make possible.

To Briony, Judith, and me it was unknown; for although Aunt Lucia had occasionally descended on us for short visits—armed with a formidable ear trumpet—she was a recluse and did not like children and we had never been invited to stay with her in Wales.

Once our father and mother went, and we were sent to stay with Mother's old nannie in her remote cottage in rural Cambridgeshire. I did not mind this, for it meant that I had precious time to read in peace. I liked the country; Briony rejoiced in pottering about in house and field and garden pursuing delights of her own; but Judith hated it and was bored and "difficult," and when Judith was difficult she let everyone know about it.

So while Briony and I with unconcealed enthusiasm looked forward to our move to Wales as if to a promised land, it did not surprise us that Judith held other views and took no pains to hide her violent opposition.

"But darling, think of all the lovely things you will be able to do," said my mother. "Riding and bathing and picnics on the beach."

To all suggestions of joys in store, Judith simply answered, "I want to stay in London!"

"But *why?*" asked my mother anxious to discover some reason for her defiant attitude.

"I just like London and want to stay here," Judith replied.

Nobody could throw any light on the matter; I knew of nothing and no person except her godmother in London to account for her attachment to the city; and in the end my father lost patience with her.

"Any more of this nonsense, miss, and you'll be packed off to boarding school," he threatened.

"I should like that," said Judith quietly.

As a matter of fact we were all "packed off to boarding school," for it was discovered that there was then no suitable school for us in that area of Pembrokeshire.

Judith was jubilant, and I could see her saying to herself, "I've won again!"

That was the terrifying thing about Judith, she always won in the end, everything always fell out just as she wanted it to—well nearly always—and of course it did this time, too, for Briony came rushing to me a few days later bristling with nine-year-old indignation.

"Liss!" she panted. "They're sending us to boarding school in *London!*"

"In London?" I repeated foolishly. "Why so far from our new home?"

It was true. My mother explained it to me a day or two later.

"You'll have the advantages of both town and country, Melissa," she said, "but more important than that, the headmistress is a cousin of Aunt Gertrude's so we can be certain that we are leaving you in good hands."

"If they are anything like Aunt Gertrude's hands, they'll be too good for me," I thought privately. Aunt Gertrude had married my mother's brother and was forever preaching at her relations; luckily we did not see her often for she lived in the north.

"Your father and I have been to see the school," my mother continued, "and it seems satisfactory in every way, much more expensive than we could have afforded up till now of course," she added.

We were to go to St. Ethelburgha's College for Young Ladies at the beginning of the following term, in a few weeks' time.

There followed an orgy of clothes-buying, which only Judith enjoyed, and soon everything was ready for our departure. Our parents would move to Newcove during our school term so it would be the Easter holidays before we even saw our new home.

Then the last night before we left for school a dreadful thing happened, which shook horribly my faith in my parents.

Briony who shared my room had already gone to bed, and Judith was sorting out her numerous tubes of paint into two piles, one to go with her to school and one to go to Pembrokeshire—Judith's painting was one of the Important Things in our family.

As I passed the boot-hole, a large dark cupboard under the stairs facing the kitchen door, I heard a sound which stopped me dead and set my heart wildly thumping, a long shuddering intake of breath ending in a sob.

For a moment I stood rooted to the spot, waiting for the sound to be repeated; we had always pretended to ourselves that the boot-hole was haunted, perhaps it really was. Then a very human sniff came from inside the cupboard, and I turned up the gas jet in the passage and pulled open the door. Huddled on the floor, as if worn out with weeping, sat the dejected figure of Emmy Lee.

I dropped onto my knees beside her and put my arms round her shoulders. "Whatever is the matter Emmy?" I asked. "What is wrong? Please tell me."

Emmy Lee gazed piteously at me and her lips began to quiver again as she whispered, "They won't let me come to Wales with you, Miss Liss, they're sending me back to the orphanage."

"What!" I exclaimed. "Who won't let you come with us? Who are sending you back to the orphanage?" As I spoke I realized that we children had never even thought of Emmy not coming with us. We had taken it completely for granted that where we went she would go too.

"The Master and Mistress, your father and mother,

Miss," she said. "They told me ever so kindly and explained that it would all be too strange to me, being so far from London and me a Londoner."

"But you do want to come with us?" I asked.

"Oh yes, Miss, more than anything in the world."

"Very well," I said grimly. "I'll go and see about it now."

I must have looked very angry for I remember Emmy muttering, "Don't take on so, Miss, perhaps it's all for the best," as I stormed along the passage and marched into the drawing room.

I don't remember what I said to my astonished parents, who really were kind people though lacking in imagination like many grownups, but they must have felt very hurt at my accusations of injustice and cruelty to an orphan. All I can remember is my repeated assertion to every explanation they made, "Emmy *must* come with us!"

At last my father gave in. "We'd better take the girl after all and put an end to all this flapdoodle," he said. "Are you sure she wants to come?"

"Certain sure," I answered and I fled back to the kitchen where Emmy had pulled herself together and was making a cup of tea.

"It's all right!" I cried throwing my arms round her. "You are coming with us, dear Emmy!"

Emmy Lee stood up to face me and took both my hands in hers, as if taking a life oath of fidelity, "I'll never leave you Miss Liss," she said, "—never!"

# CHAPTER TWO

I HAVE LITTLE IMPRESSION OF OUR FIRST TERM AT BOARD-ing school, so I think that nothing of great interest can have happened. We were just three new girls among a bunch of others, and I am sure we were quite undistinguished.

I remember that Briony was more homesick than any of us, and that Judith was the happiest of the three.

I think we all had chicken pox mildly, and I can remember the first letter I got from my mother, written on paper with our new address stamped at the head of the page:

THE OLD COURT
NEWCOVE
PEMBROKESHIRE

It was rather an exciting letter telling us about our new home.

"This is a fascinating old house to live in," she wrote, "I am sure you will love it. We have painted your room white, and one of your windows looks straight out to sea. The garden is full of primroses and early daffodils and there is a wonderful old weeping ash tree. You will be home before the leaves are out on it."

The Easter holidays came at last, and one morning in early April we boarded the train for the Pembrokeshire coast.

It was a long tedious journey, and by the time we reached the terminus and were helped into the wagonette my father had hired to meet us, our trunks and belongings stowed beside us, the first stars were beginning to pinpoint the sky.

We drove along the hilly country road, always within sight of the sea, chattering gaily to our father whom we had not seen for almost three months, till suddenly Briony fell fast asleep on my shoulder, and I realized how tired we all were.

It was nearly dark when we turned off the road and up the drive to the house, and I looked for the first time on the Old Court which was to be my home.

It was a tall old house, strongly built of stone which had been whitewashed. Its woodwork was painted

black, and it was three stories high. Lamplight shone
from the downstairs rooms, and as we clattered into the
cobbled yard at the back, my mother came running out
to welcome us, followed by dear Emmy Lee.

We were swept into the warm kitchen where we
revived enough to eat our suppers and exchange our
news, but gradually our chattering grew drowsier, and
mother led Judith and me up to our bedrooms, where
Emmy Lee had already vanished with the sleeping
Briony.

My eyelids felt like lead; I could scarcely keep my
eyes open, and I was only able to glance round my white
bedroom with approval and contentment before I tumbled into bed and fell heavily asleep.

I was aware during the night of sheets of rain battering at my windows, but I opened my eyes in the morning to sunshine and blue skies. I lay stretching happily
and looking round my sunny white room, from dressing
chest to bookcase, from escritoire to clothes cupboard.
My mother had taken a lot of trouble to paint and fur-
nish it, and it was charming. I had windows on three
sides; from east and west I could look on sunrise and
sunset, and behind me to the north at the sea. I was
suddenly out of bed and gazing through the round window to the north, round like a porthole, like an eye
blinking across the blue water of the bay.

I was astonished, for I had not thought the house tall
enough to glimpse the sea across nearly a mile of fields.

I dressed quickly and hurried across the passage to
Judith's room. I found it empty; she had evidently begun

her exploration of the house ahead of me. I saw that her window looked down onto an exceedingly old tree, its branches twisted into fantastic shapes—it must be the weeping ash that mother had mentioned in her letter.

Briony, on the floor below us and next to Emmy Lee, was still snugly asleep, curled up small like a mouse. She awoke as I tiptoed out of her room, and I waited while she dressed and plaited her hair.

By the time the gong sounded for breakfast, we had all made a cursory tour of the house, but it took us the rest of those holidays and several others to really get to know it, and to discover all of its secret places.

We were a gay party at the breakfast table in the cozy low-beamed dining room next to the kitchen. The wide old fireplace had been filled in to a reasonable size, and a wood fire crackled merrily on the hearth.

We could hardly wait till the end of breakfast to get on with our exploration, and to savor the first smells and sounds and sights of this enchanting place.

"No tasks today," Mother announced. "You may get yourselves unpacked and sorted out and get to know our new home a little."

Our "tasks" were allotted to each of us every week by Mother. Sometimes it was arranging the flowers, sometimes counting and putting away the clean linen, or washing the second best china and standing it back in its cupboard. My mother always did the best herself.

"Shall we help Emmy Lee clear the table," I suggested. But my mother assured me that there were two good women who came in daily from the village to help in the house, both called Mrs. Evans, and differentiated by their husbands' trades, so that they were known as Mrs. Evans the Forge, and Mrs. Evans the Cobbler. Both were dark comfortable women, both were equally aimiable to us, but Mrs. Evans the Forge became our favorite for we loved to visit her husband and watch him at work at his fiery furnace, while the docile farm horses stood patiently by, waiting to be shod.

My father had stepped happily into the shoes of a country doctor, and after breakfast we went through the back door of the house and reached the cobbled yard and across it to the stables and outhouses, where a dark young man stood waiting with the doctor's dogcart ready for him to go on his rounds.

"Rees Owen, these are my daughters, Melissa, Judith and Briony," said my father, and the tall young man touched his cap in greeting. I liked his open face and his shy smile, and felt I would get on well with the Welsh.

My father kissed us good-by, clattered out of the yard and down the lane to the coast road, and we returned to the house, and our unpacking.

Never were trunks emptied so quickly. The clothes were neatly stored in cupboard and drawer, and then we were ready to resume our tour of inspection.

On the top floor there was a guest room between the attic bedrooms belonging to Judith and me; on the second were my parents' room, Briony's and Emmy Lee's little room, and on the ground floor apart from the kitchen and the dining room, there was a sunny drawing

room, low-ceilinged and painted white, and a smaller
room that might be called a study. But beyond the
kitchen lay the oldest part of the house, three hundred
years old my father said. Here one stepped into another
world, an ancient world of hidden mysteries imprisoned
in the solid stone walls, a shadowy world, eerie, brood-
ing and threatening. Here prisoners must have awaited
their trial—footpads, thieves, highwaymen, even witches.
Here they must have been imprisoned in the days when
the courts of law were held in the house, long long ago.
And here they had left their evil shadow so that one
could still smell wickedness and despair after all those
years. I dared not linger here. I was too much afraid of
seeing one of those old unhappy ghosts.

My father had whitewashed this place and used it as
an office—his surgery was in the village.

Leading up out of it were worn wooden stairs, which
mounted to the loft, dark and low-raftered, a place of
infinite possibilities but again impregnated with the same
eeriness I had felt down below. I determined to come
here as little as possible. I was glad to escape out-of-doors
to where, hidden behind the thick old wall that enclosed
them, house and garden communed together; for the
normal entry to the house was through the cobbled yard
round at the back. To reach the front door, one had to
go through a little gate in the encircling wall, which shut
off house and garden from the inquisitive eye.

It was not a large garden and it was mostly given over
to the orchard of apple, pear and cherry trees. There was
an old summerhouse, and a stone gardeners' shed the

home of several robins, and one well-kept little lawn surrounded by neat borders full of clumps of flowers stirring towards spring. Jasmine and rose clung to the rough stones of the wall, preparing for a riot of color and scent in the summer months ahead. Everywhere under the fruit trees daffodils tossed their golden heads, bending before the harsh sea wind in spite of the sheltering wall.

But the outstanding feature of the garden was without doubt the extraordinary old weeping ash, which I had first seen from Judith's window. It grew quite close to the house, and its highest branches were on a level with the roof. I felt, from the size of its great trunk, that it should have risen high above the chimneys, stretching aloft its lacy fingers towards the sky, but instead of this it was shrunken and contorted like an aged woman whose limbs are crippled with rheumatism.

Later on, in the summer holidays, we made wonderful houses in the branches of the old tree, where the drowsy hum of the bees came up to us as we played, our faces patterned with the sunlit leaves.

We soon settled down into our new home and each day of those first holidays was filled with fresh discoveries and surprises.

# CHAPTER THREE

IN THE FAR CORNER OF OUR GARDEN THERE WAS A LITTLE wicket gate that opened onto the fields. A path led across them to a stile over a stone wall, and beyond that, sheltering in a fold of the hills, there stood a gray cottage. We were intrigued with it from the start and began to people it with creatures of our imagination, so it was quite a shock one morning to see, from the branches of the weeping ash where we were playing, a woman leave the cottage and come briskly along the path from the stile and into our garden through our gate. We waited hidden till she had made her way round to the back of the house, passing under our hiding place, then we scrambled down and shot through the front door to find out from Emmy Lee who she was.

"Why Mrs. Owen, of course," said Emmy, "come to do the washing. You'll find her in the wash house."

Later we sought her out where she stood, her arms deep in steaming wooden tubs of soap suds, scrubbing and rubbing at piles of underclothes and linen. She greeted us shyly and invited us to come to her cottage when we liked. I always thought of a hedgehog when I saw her, perhaps because of her hands permanently pink and wrinkled with hot water, and her quick black eyes which missed nothing.

And yet . . . and yet, there was something odd about her. I recognized from the first day I saw her, some strange isolation of spirit that placed her apart. The other village women avoided her, and when I mentioned Mrs. Rees Owen the usual response was a shrug of the shoulders and an "Oh, her," which never got me anywhere. They spoke of her as "that one," and I noticed that the other women did not come to work in the house on Mondays when she was there. It was all very strange and intriguing, and I wondered whether in the old days she would have been branded as a witch, for she claimed to have "the sight," to be able to foresee the future.

Mrs. Owen was the wife of Old Rees our gardener, and mother of Young Rees, whom we had first met with my father's dogcart the morning after our arrival. He was handyman about the place, and one never knew where one would meet him next.

One day we visited his mother's cottage. I was taken

by surprise when he walked into the kitchen where we were enjoying a plateful of Mrs. Owen's Welsh cakes. I remember how embarrassed he looked at finding us there, and to cover his discomfort I admired the early blooms on a bush of yellow tea roses, growing on the sheltered wall outside the cottage window. Immediately he leaned over the sill and picked one for me and one for Briony, and as we walked home across the field I stuck mine in my hair.

Judith had not come with us and expressed astonishment that we enjoyed the "company of the servants," as she said. But I never thought of these people as our servants, they were my friends.

Gradually Judith began to detach herself from Briony and me. She dropped out of our games and hid herself away, withdrawing from us into a secret life of her own. She had always been "different," and now she began to take a pride in being so. Where she spent her time and what she did during the holidays I cannot remember, but she came punctually to meals and joined all the family outings and gatherings. It was only from our private world as children, that she was absent.

I remember after supper one summer night Briony and I crossed the fields towards the coast. My parents had gone to spend the evening with friends, I think, and Judith sat finishing a painting in the garden. Emmy Lee, of course, could not be persuaded to leave the house and come with us. We took a path round the edge of the cliffs and came to a spur of rock, which ran out into the sea and sheltered on one side our favorite bathing beach. Something prompted Briony to peer down into the sea. I have not a good head for heights, so although I kept a firm hold on Briony's skirt, I did not peep myself.

"Oh, Liss! You must look! It's a wonderful place!" cried Briony. So on all fours I crawled up over the rough grass and peered down over the edge. A tiny rocky cove of deep water lay below us, hemmed in by cliffs, and from the boom and smack of the swell I knew there must be a cave.

"Come on," said Briony. "We must go and see," and she jumped up and led the way down through a crack between the rocks to a platform. Terrified, I followed her, for I dared not let her go alone. Beyond us we saw a narrow ledge, and cut steps descending to a lower platform. Briony insisted on going down them. "Look!" she cried. "They must be smugglers' steps—somebody has cut them out of the rock; they are well worn too. Come on, I'll help you," she urged.

So I allowed myself to be persuaded, and gingerly, hugging the rock face, I made the horrible descent and flopped thankfully onto the spacious platform beneath. Now we were much nearer to the water, and I could imagine in a storm how easily one could be swept off by the waves into the sea. Safely on a firm base, I was able to relax and look around me with pleasure. It was a wonderfully hidden and secret place, and Briony felt certain that no one but us had rediscovered it since it was last used by smugglers.

"What did they smuggle?" she asked.

"Brandy . . . from France, perhaps," I suggested.

We sat serene and happy, watching the sky turn to
flame and the red sun dipping towards the sea, while the
seagulls wheeled and cried over the bay.

Suddenly, from somewhere below our feet, a desolate
moaning broke out, shattering our peace. We jumped
to our feet in alarm and clung together as the cry rose
and fell like an anguished sobbing.

"Somebody's hurt!" I gulped. "Someone has fallen
down there and can't get up! Oh! Oh! how dreadful!
Quick, Briony, we must run and get help."

We peered anxiously down at the water but could
see nothing, so with Briony leading the way, we fled up
the smugglers' steps, scrambled through the crack out
onto the cliff, and began to tear along the path towards
the nearest farm.

We had not gone far, however, when we saw a man
sitting on the stile, and to our infinite relief, as we got
nearer, we saw that it was Young Rees.

We threw ourselves at him, pulling him off the stile in
our agitation, both of us panting so hard we could barely
speak.

"Quick! Someone's hurt down in the cove. Bring a
rope, or a boat. Oh, quickly! Quickly! We heard them
moaning. It was terrible!"

"Which cove? Where?" asked Rees anxiously.

I pointed along the way we had come.

"There, that one. Where the smugglers' steps are!"
I cried, "Oh, please hurry. We may be too late!"

But Rees, who had for a moment looked alarmed, was
grinning broadly.

"Was this the noise?" he asked, and he produced an excellent imitation of the moaning that had frightened us so.

"Yes, yes!" we cried, impatiently. "But you must do something, quickly!"

To our amazement, the grin on Rees' face broadened as he said quietly, "There's nothing to worry about. No one is hurt. What you heard is the song of the seals."

"The seals?" I gasped. "Do you mean to tell me that there are seals in the cove?"

He nodded, chuckling at my astonishment.

"Yes," he said. "Haven't you seen our seals yet, Miss Liss? Come back now with me and I'll show you."

I looked at Briony, hesitating. It was long past her bedtime, but this was a chance not to be missed.

"All right," I agreed. "But we mustn't stay too long."

"I'll take you both home, Miss, afterwards," Rees promised, and he took Briony's hand. We walked back to the crack in the cliff, scrambled down it, and then went by the steps to the lower platform. There we sat in silence, listening and waiting for what seemed ages. Suddenly Rees stiffened and whispered, "Look." As I gazed down into the water below, I saw a round head bob up, followed by a second, and third—a family of seals were swimming lazily about, a stone's throw away from us.

We lay perfectly still, scarcely daring to breathe, and after a few minutes they disappeared and we heard the moaning song again. Then they were back, swimming to and fro in the tiny cove.

We watched them till it was almost dark and the wind from the sea began to get chilly, then Rees took us back by a short cut skirting the cliffs. "Don't ever come this way after a storm," he warned us. "The cliff is being undermined by the sea and this path is treacherous. There is always the danger of a landslide after heavy rain."

The lamps were lit in the house when we got back, and Emmy Lee was out in the drive with a lantern anxiously scanning the darkening fields.

"Here we are," I cried. "Rees is with us. We're all right." Emmy soon forgave us when she heard our story, especially when we promised to take her to Seal Cove next time we went there.

One night soon after this, a wild storm blew up that lasted for three days. The wind screamed and howled round our chimneys and the tall trees bent before it like grasses. Out in the bay the few hardy fishing boats tossed on the waves like match sticks, and the surf roared against the rocks sending the spray high over the headlands. We had to stay in the house during the violent bouts of rain, and it was during one of these times that Briony unearthed trouble.

Judith had locked herself into her room on the top floor and sat engrossed in her drawing.

I had found a wonderful collection of old books belonging to Aunt Lucia in the bookshelves of the study. One of them was a tome on witchcraft, and I found it fascinating. I gloated over some of its weird incantations and instructions.

"Draw a full circle counter-clockwise."

"Dance widdershins on Allhallows Eve."

"There must be fire within the circle; light a candle in the room."

A delicious shiver of fear ran up my spine as I read, although I took it all as a joke. I had no reason to do otherwise.

Briony spent this time poking about in the old loft over Father's office. She had wanted to for some time, but Judith discouraged her from going there. She looked upon this place as her territory because she found it first; and it was not worth a scene. However, while Judith was engrossed in her work on the top floor, Briony was able to slip away and spend a blissful afternoon burrowing and delving in the old leather trunks, wicker baskets, tin cases and general junk with which the attic was stacked.

I thought at tea that Briony wore a secret look of excitement, but it was not till bedtime, when I went to say goodnight to her, that she told me what she had found. She was sitting up in bed, her eyes bright, her face flushed, and something was clutched tightly to her under the bedclothes. "Look what I've got," said Briony proudly, and she held towards me a slim wooden doll.

I sat down on the bed and put out my hands to take her, but a feeling of such strong revulsion swept over me that I drew back loath to touch her.

But Briony laid the doll on my knee, and after a moment my curiosity overcame my dislike and I began to remove the old vest in which she was wrapped, to examine her more closely.

The doll looked ageless, and I suspected she was very old indeed, for she was polished and smooth like a chestnut with the caresses of many hands. Her arms and legs were attached to her body with iron pins and swung freely though solidly. She was unpainted. Her hair and features were beautifully carved and her expression was a curious mixture—wise, sly, enigmatic, and to me entirely unpleasant, almost frightening. She was made of very hard wood, holly wood perhaps, and she had few marks or scratches on her; but down her back, gouged out of her spine, were the letters D I D O.

"D-i-d-o, Dido," I whispered. "Dido must be her name. Where on earth did you find her, Briony?"

"In the old loft, at the bottom of a leather trunk," said Briony. "She is mine and I love her." Fiercely she seized the doll from me and rewrapped her in the vest, fondling the unyielding creature against her cheek.

"Judith will be furious," I warned her. "She looks upon that attic and everything in it as hers, and she'll be angry that she didn't find this doll herself. You'll have to hide it."

"I know," Briony retorted. "And you're not to tell her, Liss. Only you and Emmy Lee know about Dido. She is *my* secret, *mine!*"

I kissed Briony good night and went to my room feeling disturbed; there was something horrible about the wooden doll, something menacing. I would like to have taken it at once down to the kitchen stove and thrown it into the flames.

# CHAPTER FOUR

WHEN THE HOLIDAYS CAME TO AN END AND IT WAS TIME to go back to school, Briony had not decided what to do with Dido. She was so miserable at the thought of leaving her behind that she wanted to take the creature back to school with her and keep it hidden in a locker or drawer.

"But I daren't," said Briony. "Someone would be sure to discover her, and somehow Judith would hear about it."

"Does Dido matter so much to you?" I asked.

"Yes, yes, she does, she's *mine*, and I love her," cried Briony hysterically.

In the end, with great reluctance, she gave the doll to

Emmy Lee to keep for her, and I hoped that by the next holidays Briony might have forgotten her.

However, it was just the opposite; Dido's spell or fascination, call it what you will, seemed stronger than ever, and Briony herself began to change, she became secretive and touchy, even spiteful, and liable to sudden flares of temper.

And then the inevitable happened.

Judith had set off after lunch to see an artist friend who lived on "the mountain" above Newcove, and I had promised Briony to cut out a new frock for Dido while Judith was out of the house. Emmy Lee provided the "piece" bag, and we spread out, in gorgeous array, silks, satins, muslins, rags, bits of material left from our family dressmaking over the years.

Briony chose a piece of wonderful jade-green satin, remnant of an evening dress of my mother's. I cut it out and fitted it on Dido, my mouth crammed full of pins while Emmy Lee stood watching critically.

"It makes that old doll look almost human," she said teasingly.

"What . . . doll?"

The drawling words were spoken very quietly, and we all jumped guiltily. Judith was standing in the open doorway.

For a moment nobody spoke and she repeated her question, "What . . . doll?" The words fell on the still-ness like icy drops into a pool. I removed the pins from my mouth and stammered, "I . . . I thought you had g-gone out?"

"So I had," Judith replied. "And now I am back."

I could see that she was blazingly angry, and in a moment she strode across the room and took the doll out of Briony's protecting arms.

Then the storm broke. Briony flew at her hitting, scratching, biting, kicking, and tearing at Judith's hair— I was horrified. She had never behaved like this before. "She's mine! Dido is mine!" she screamed.

"Stop it at once, Briony," I shouted, and Emmy Lee threw her arms round the struggling little girl and carried her bodily out of the room.

Judith turned to me, a half-amused smile curling her cold lips.

"What an exhibition," she remarked.

I held out my hand for the doll.

"Briony adores the creature," I said. "You mustn't pay too much attention to her outburst."

Judith shrugged her shoulders and turned the doll about examining her minutely. I saw her eyes flash avidly for a second and I knew that the doll appealed to her.

"There is a certain fascination about her, you know. She is really rather beautiful, and unusual," said Judith in a deliberately calm tone.

"How did Briony get her?"

"She found her," I replied shortly.

"Found her? Where?"

I hesitated and then replied firmly, "I shan't tell you where."

"Don't bother," said Judith coolly. "I can guess. In the loft wasn't it? I told Briony to keep out of there."

And she handed Dido back to me.

No more was said at the time, and when Judith and Briony met at supper there was no apparent trace of trouble between them; but I knew it was not the end of the matter, and I also knew that somehow Judith would secure Dido for herself.

A week or two passed and then Briony came to me sobbing convulsively.

"Dido has gone!" she cried. "I c-c-can't find her. She's lost."

"How do you mean gone?" I asked.

"Disappeared. Vanished," said Briony. "I left her in my tree house after breakfast, in the hole in the trunk. I'm *sure* I did, and when I went back she wasn't there. It's that beastly Judith! She has taken her, I know she has!"

"Have you looked carefully? Could she have fallen down somehow?" I asked. Briony shook her head. She was inconsolable, and after a few days she began to look so peaked that even my mother noticed, and threatened to send her to old Nannie in Cambridgeshire for a change of air.

I asked Judith about Dido, but she professed to know nothing about her, and the strange thing was that on the day of Dido's disappearance Judith had been away all day with her artist friend. How had she stolen the doll? How could she have managed it? For I was convinced that somehow she had spirited Dido away. Briony never saw the doll again.

I wanted to tell my parents the whole story, but in our

family there was a strong tradition that we kept grown-ups out of our children's world, out of our concerns and our troubles. It was partly that our parents were so much wrapped up in each other that they did not become involved with us and we were careful not to intrude on them. Emmy Lee, of course, we counted not as a grownup but as one of ourselves. So I said nothing, and it was Emmy Lee not our parents who brought comfort to Briony. On one of her infrequent expeditions to the village she returned with a gray Persian kitten in her shopping basket, and Dido's place in Briony's affection was quickly filled. She soon became her normal pleasant self once more.

The months passed by, and soon it was spring again and the Easter holidays.

Briony and I were at home on our own, since Judith had gone straight from school to her godmother in London. We were relaxed and happy in a lighthearted way that was not possible when Judith was in the house.

A favorite walk of ours was up on the moors behind Mrs. Owen's cottage, where the lovely spring call of the curlews came bubbling up to us from the reed beds where they nested.

One evening in April, Briony and I had wandered across the heather, stopping every few minutes to look for nests or peer at some tiny creature scuttling into cover. We were returning down the hill towards Mrs. Owen's cottage, our eyes fixed on the blue smoke of our own chimneys beyond, when we stopped dead in our tracks, halted by the most odd sound—the moaning we had heard in the cove. We looked at one another incredulously.

"Seals," breathed Briony.

"It can't be," I whispered. "We're much too far inland."

We resumed our way, treading lightly, our ears attentive, and presently it came again, the same sound but nearer, and unmistakably—seals.

"Where?" I asked. "Where does the noise come from?"

"Perhaps someone keeps a pet seal?" Briony suggested, and strange fancies of possible underground inlets of the sea flitted through my mind. But as we descended further the mystery was intensified, for, unbelievably, the noise was coming from Mrs. Owen's cottage.

It was the same low wailing moan which had so startled us that time we heard it at Seal Cove. The song of the seals.

"Why, it is Rees doing an imitation of a seal for fun," I said laughing, but Briony shook her head and nodded to a place across a couple of fields where we could see Rees ploughing for Mr. Jenkins.

We looked at one another round-eyed as we crept towards the cottage, while the sound rose and fell, growing louder as we approached it.

Rather quietly, for one does not spy on a friend, and Mrs. Owen was our friend, we tiptoed to the window and peeped in.

There was no one there but Mrs. Owen. Old Rees must have been at "The Sailor's Return," chatting with his friends over a mug of beer.

She sat by the kitchen fire knitting and rocking herself gently backwards and forwards to her strange crooning seal song.

We backed away from the window, embarrassed and a little frightened.

"Is she mad?" Briony asked anxiously.

"Well, no, I don't think so," I assured her, "but she is certainly behaving very oddly."

I remembered the silences that had fallen on the village women when Mrs. Owen's name was mentioned, how people called her queer, and I began to wonder if there could be any truth in the old stories I had heard of seal men and women: human beings who at times took the forms of seals and lived for a season with those animals around the rocky coasts.

We stood hesitating, wondering what to do. It was so very peculiar. Should we go in and see Mrs. Owen, or should we pass by in silence?

"We must go in and make sure she is all right," I whispered. "We can always fetch Rees if she's . . . if need be." It was all very odd, and I must say I felt a little frightened.

"Come on," I said, plucking up my courage.

So we walked boldly to the back door and knocked, and waited. The sound stopped at once, but there was no movement.

"It's us, Mrs. Owen," I called. There was the noise of a chair scraping on flagstones, and Mrs. Owen opened the door and stood blinking at us. She looked perfectly

normal, her usual genial self.

"Come in," she invited. "Come in and sit down and warm yourselves."

We sat down feeling rather foolish, and at a loss for something to say. But Mrs. Owen appeared not to notice and chattered away about nothing in particular.

After a while we left for home, and met Young Rees plodding home for his supper. He stood aside to let us pass on the narrow path across the fields.

"We've been to see your mother," I said. Should I mention what we had heard? Better not, it would only embarrass him, and he was shy enough anyway. We'd have to wait and "contain our souls in patience," as Emmy Lee said, till we found the explanation of Mrs.

Owen's strange behavior.

On the last Sunday afternoon before we went back to school, Briony and I went down to Seal Cove. As we climbed down to our usual perch, we were surprised to hear the sound of music very near us. We peered over the edge of our platform and saw before us, on a spur of rock uncovered by the low tide, Young Rees sitting, playing his mouth organ. I was about to call to him, as he was too much absorbed to notice us, when I saw, bobbing about in the water close to him, the round heads of three or four seals. They appeared to be listening to the music. As we watched, fascinated, they approached nearer. Rees went on playing for some time, and we were beginning to grow cramped in our stillness, when a diving gull made him look up, and he saw us and stopped. Immediately the bobbing heads disappeared and Rees, rather shamefacedly, climbed up to our platform. "Good afternoon Miss Liss, Miss Briony," he stammered, and I felt that we had been trespassing in his private world.

"Sit down beside us, Rees, won't you?" I invited. "We couldn't let you know we were here without disturbing the seals. I hope you don't mind? I had no idea you were a magician!"

He laughed shyly, but I saw that he was pleased with the compliment.

"Magician!" he exclaimed. "That's nothing! You should hear my mother. Why she can draw the seals from every cove round this coast by calling to them in their own language."

So that was it. Briony and I exchanged a look of relief.

"We heard her practicing one day in the cottage," I confessed, "and we wondered."

Rees laughed, his shyness forgotten.

"No wonder folks think her a queer one," he said. "But she is as good as any doctor, with animals that is. They trust her; she has the gentle hand, you see."

"The gentle hand," I repeated thoughtfully. It was a delightful expression, and I said to myself, "If ever I am badly hurt, I will remember to send for Mrs. Owen."

# CHAPTER FIVE

THE SEASONS SLID QUIETLY BY, SCHOOL HOLIDAYS SUC-
ceeding one another, and at the end of each one we felt
more closely drawn into the life of the Old Court and
loved it even better. We were well known in the district
because of my father and had many friends among the
country people, but we led a strangely isolated life. We
seldom met young people. Most of our parents' friends
were retired couples whose families were grownup and
had left home. But we were deeply happy, Briony and I,
and although my mother worrried at times at our lack
of social activities, we were perfectly contented.

With Judith it was different. She had never pretended

to enjoy the country, and her preference for London became more marked as she grew older. Her godmother was always pleased to have her stay in her tall house in Knightsbridge, and it came to be the recognized thing that Judith only spent part of each holiday at home.

I wonder now how my parents failed to see the gulf that was opening between Judith and the rest of us, a gulf that grew deeper and wider each year, one that we could not cross. Although she was our sister, Briony and I knew little of the real person who lived behind her cold beautiful face. I think, even our parents, though they never said anything, must have felt this barrier. Judith was in the family but not of it. I often tried during our school years to cross the gulf and make friends with her, but always she repulsed me and retired behind her mask, secretive and detached, keeping her isolation. I think it was because she was unable to love anyone, even then.

I was sixteen when I first met Carew. He was stretched full length along the edge of the farm track as I came along it on my way to buy some eggs. Our hens had stopped laying for some reason. At first I thought he was hurt, and then I saw that he was drawing, with utter absorption, a tiny shrew that sat cleaning his whiskers, balanced on a tuft of grass. The little creature jumped down and began to search about on the ground for something to eat. And in a moment he had done two or three rough pencil sketches of it with a few decisive lines. Suddenly with a whisk of its tail the shrew vanished and the boy rolled over on his side with a grunt of annoyance and saw me.

"Hello?" he said with a friendly grin. "How long have you been standing there?"

"I didn't want to disturb the shrew," I explained, "not till you'd finished. Your drawings are rather good, you know."

He went pink in the face.

"Oh, d'you think so?" he exclaimed. "I can do much better than that. Are you staying at the farm?"

"No," I replied, "I live here, at Newcove, I mean. I'm just going to the farm for some eggs."

He came with me and carried the basket back as far as the road. I learned his name, Carew Grenville, and that he came to spend his holidays at Penbryn, Sir David Grenville's house, on the far side of Newcove from us.

"Uncle David is my guardian," Carew told me, "since my parents were killed in a car accident a year ago. He is my father's eldest brother, you see, and has no children of his own, so I am his heir. Some day Penbryn will be mine."

"And have you no family, no brothers or sisters I mean?" I asked.

"None, there's only me," he said simply, and my heart warmed to him.

"I'm sorry," I said, "but you must have lots of friends."

He shook his head.

"Not here," he said. "I know nobody, and my uncle and aunt are rather . . . well . . . elderly."

We laughed together, in complete understanding.

Once I had accompanied my father on a visit to Penbryn, a gaunt forbidding old house, shut away in its de-
cayed splendor. Sir David found it hard to make ends
meet and to keep the house in the family; there had been
Grenvilles at Penbryn for three hundred years. He and
Lady Grenville were seldom seen outside their own
grounds, and I wondered what kind of life a boy of
about my age would lead with them.

"I am Melissa Mansell," I said. "You must come and
meet my family. I have two sisters; one of them paints
rather well. That's our house," and I pointed across the
fields to the Old Court.

We parted at the end of the farm track where he had
left his bicycle. He shook hands with me a little for-
mally and rode off whistling gaily.

I planned as I walked home how I was to see him
again, for see him I must. Could I ask my mother to
invite him to tea, or should I ask to accompany her when
next she called at Penbryn?

The matter was solved for me by a puncture a few
days later. I found Carew on the roadside near our lane,
with a flat tire and no pump, and I invited him to come
up to the house to borrow a pump and mend his tire.

I knew that only Briony and Emmy Lee were at home;
Judith was still away, and my mother out at one of her
afternoon meetings.

He set the bicycle upside down on the cobbles outside
the kitchen door, and I fetched him a basin of water and
my father's bicycle pump.

Briony and Emmy Lee, who were shelling peas in the

porch, came out to meet him, and when I said, "You'll
stay for tea in the kitchen, won't you?" he accepted
readily and Emmy Lee disappeared into the house to
make some scones.

We had almost finished eating when there was a tap
at the door and Mrs. Owen popped her head in. She
often dropped in for a cup of tea with Emmy. She would
not come in at first when she saw that Emmy was not
alone, but we insisted, and after tea we persuaded her
to read our tea cups.

Most of it was the usual nonsense, dark strangers, long
journeys, crossing water, and we had a lot of fun over
it. But when last of all it came to my turn, Mrs. Owen
stiffened and a change came over her.

"I can't see anything in your cup, Miss Melissa," she
said, "it's . . . too hard for me!" and after a few minutes
she made an excuse and hurried away. What had she
seen in my cup that she would not tell me?

Later I took Carew round the garden and through
the wicket gate across the fields, past Mrs. Owen's cottage to my favorite spot on the moor; I told him about
the curlews, and we listened to them as we sat together
enraptured with one another.

All too soon he had to go, for his uncle was strict
about his being punctual for dinner. Just before he left
me, at the gate into the orchard, he put his hand into his
pocket and drew out a slightly crumpled piece of paper.

"Melissa, this is for you," he said shyly. "That is to
say if you would like it."

I took it from him, exclaiming in delight at the finished

drawing of the shrew. It was most delicately done in pencil, and so realistic that I could feel the warm fur nestling in my hand.

"Oh, thank you," I cried. "Of course I'd love to have it. How I wish I could draw like you."

When I reached the house, I ran upstairs to my room and laid the drawing carefully away in the secret drawer of my escritoire.

I washed my hair later that evening and sat drying it beside the kitchen fire while Emmy Lee brushed it for me and we gossiped together.

"That's a proper young man, Miss Liss," she commented, "handsome too, and thinks the world of you."

"Oh, Emmy," I cried, "do you really think so? I wish I could believe you. Do you think he really likes me?"

"Of course he does," said Emmy.

"You won't tell anyone, will you, Emmy? Promise. About Carew and me. Nobody." (I meant Judith of course.) "I couldn't bear for anyone else to know, except Briony and she's too young to understand."

Emmy Lee nodded solemnly.

"I promise," she said softly and a warm blush crept over her face.

"I know just how you feel, Miss Liss."

"Oh Emmy!" I cried. "You too? There is someone you are fond of? I'm so glad. Who is he?"

She shook her head and began to brush my hair more vigorously, so I did not press for an answer.

The friendship ripened that summer between Carew and me. Scarcely a day passed when we did not see one another. Briony had made friends with some visitors at the Jenkins' farm so I did not feel I was neglecting her.

And then Judith came home, more elegant and self-assured than I remembered her, and even more beautiful.

I had felt a slight uneasiness all along about the meeting between Judith and Carew, and now this anxiety increased. I did not trust Judith and feared that she might entice Carew away from me. How nasty, how mean and small minded I sound. But there was need to be on guard so far as Judith was concerned; I had learned from painful experience to be wary of her. She coveted what belonged to someone else.

However, after the first two or three encounters I relaxed, for Judith behaved well and did not show much interest in Carew. He confessed to me that although he found her beauty disturbing, she frightened him with her cold green eyes, which seemed to gimlet into his brain and read his very thoughts. I can best describe it by saying that there was a feeling of unease between them. Since both were artistic, I imagined that their drawing would be a bond between them, but it was not so. Rather it divided them, accentuating a basic difference in character. Carew's delicate, gentle, and infinitely careful drawing contrasted strangely with Judith's brilliant, bold, rather cruel work.

I had not seen Judith's pictures for some time, and when, one wet afternoon, I found her going through her portfolio, I was astonished to see how she had progressed. I thought her drawings amazingly well done, though I did not like them. I was shocked at the clever twist she could give to an ordinary face, making it malignant, the slight contortion which made a limb grotesque. She was able to warp and distort kindly things into monstrosities. There was no beauty in her creations, and I asked her why she must make everything harsh, ugly.

"It's the different way I see things," she said. "So much more interesting"—and there was a peculiar pride in her expression as she looked at me, with a hint of patronage.

Just then my mother called me and I ran downstairs to see what she wanted.

When I returned, Judith had vanished with her portfolio, but lying in the passage was a big envelope. I picked it up and pulled out the contents unsuspectingly.

Six drawings confronted me, six brilliant pieces of work, excellent portraits . . . of the wooden doll, Dido.

They were subtle and clever and altogether repellent. I felt the same revulsion for them as I had for the real Dido, and there was something else that Judith had caught in the expression—wickedness.

"How could a doll be wicked?" I asked myself. I tried to shrug off the feeling as a piece of fanciful nonsense, but as I stared at the horrible drawings, I realized why I had instinctively disliked the creature from the very first sight of her. The doll was wicked, evil, and I wished more than ever that I had burned her in the kitchen stove when I had the chance. Now I knew for certain that Judith must have the doll, hidden away in some place of concealment. Those drawings, minutely observed, could not have been done from memory.

My first reaction was to take the drawings to her and beg her to give me the doll so that I could rid us of it forever. With anyone but Judith this is what I would have done; but with her nothing was straightforward and easy, and I dreaded her vindictiveness when her anger was roused, for one never knew how she would strike. So despising myself for my timidity, I left the envelope where I had found it and said nothing to anyone. I retreated down to the kitchen to the comforting presence of Emmy Lee, and later on, when I passed along the passage again, the envelope had vanished.

With Carew, I had not discussed Judith nor my feelings towards her, but on one of the last days of those holidays, when we had taken a picnic down to Seal Cove and lay munching contentedly, he suddenly said, "She's a misfit, isn't she; Judith I mean."

"She has always been different from Briony and me," I answered, "and much cleverer."

"Yes, dear Liss. Much cleverer at getting her own way and taking what she wants," he said. "She has the brilliance of a diamond, and no heart. She fascinates and terrifies me. She has great magnetism and I feel she might compel me to do something against my will, something devilish, something *she* wanted."

I felt the bright day darken as he spoke, and a shiver of presentiment dimmed the magic of that well-loved spot so that I wanted to leave at once.

"Let's go and see Mrs. Owen before you go home," I suggested. "She has a young owl roosting in the tree by her cottage. You might draw it."

But Mrs. Owen was in a cantankerous mood, unusual for her, and I wondered what had upset her. She did not invite us into the cottage and the looks she cast on Carew were almost malignant. I could think of no reason for her dislike of him, and I was still puzzled over her refusal to read my tea cup.

We said good-by, Carew and I, almost lightheartedly for we had promised to write to one another and we knew we would meet again at Christmas time. In a few days trunks were packed and we were off back to school.

## CHAPTER SIX

A MONTH OR SO AFTER MY EIGHTEENTH BIRTHDAY I LEFT St. Ethelburgha's College for good and put my hair up, which was then the recognized sign that I had entered the grownup world.

Now my parents had to decide what was to be done with me. For myself I was perfectly content to stay quietly at home in Newcove waiting for Carew, reading, sewing and learning to run a home smoothly. Also I wanted to help my father by keeping his accounts in order.

"But you must have young society, Melissa," my mother insisted. "How are you going to find a husband in this remote spot?"

I'm afraid I did not take her concern very seriously.
Carew and I meant to marry sometime the following
year when he was twenty-one, after he came down
from Oxford—it was as simple as that. There would be
no difficulty in finding work, and in any case by then
he would have inherited some money from his father.
Later on Penbryn, too, would be his.

But we had not yet told my parents, so my mother
kept on trying to make plans for my future. I was to go
to a finishing school in Switzerland, or to spend six
months with distant relations in Italy, or to dance my
way with other debutantes through a London season.

I did not encourage her in any of those plans. I was
not at all anxious to do any of those things. I knew that
in the end none of them would come off, and I would
be left in peace to enjoy myself in my own way. It
worked out just as I had anticipated. My mother's burst
of energy lapsed, and I found myself at home, my days
filled pleasantly and usefully in the house and garden.
I also began, regularly, to accompany my father on some
of his calls and to lend a hand in any emergency, and
in this way I got to know better many of his poorer
patients.

Rather to my annoyance, Judith persuaded my parents to allow her to leave school a term or two after me,
and her godmother promised to take her to Paris in the
autumn, and to make all the arrangements for her to go
on with her painting there under a good teacher.

She came home for only a few weeks that summer,
to say good-by, and I remember helping to pack some of

the lovely new clothes her godmother had bought for her in London.

"What an exciting time you'll have," I said to her, "lots of parties and gaieties. Is that what you like?"

Judith shook her head. "That's not what I want," she said. "It is all too easy when one is beautiful. I need a challenge. Something that is hard to do—even impossible."

"Perhaps you'll become a great artist," I said, "and people will come from all over the world to see your pictures."

She smiled at that and her green eyes blazed.

"Yes, yes!" she cried, "and I shall paint to shock and frighten them, wicked pictures, but so fascinating that they will have to come back to look again."

Her eyes met mine and I wondered if she was thinking of those drawings she had made of Dido; and I also wondered not for the first time, if she knew that I had seen them.

Characteristically, she could not resist one last venomous jab the day before she left home.

It was early October, and the golden light that had lain all day on tree and field was fading into mist, which foretold an early frost.

Carew had come over for supper—Briony was already back at school. He and Judith and I had gathered in the warm kitchen, where Emmy Lee was rolling out pastry for an apple pie, and I was peeling the apples for her. A brisk step rang across the yard and Young Rees passed the window, knocked at the door, and deposited outside it a large basket of apples he had just picked.

Emmy Lee leaped to the door, but Carew was there before her and lifted the basket inside, while Rees in his shy way slipped off and would not be persuaded to join us.

They were enormous Bramleys, their skins a rosy red, rosy as Emmy's cheeks as she returned to the kitchen table.

"Hard luck, Emmy," Judith drawled. "But it's useless, you know. He has no eyes for anyone but Melissa."

I looked from Carew, who had gone quite white, to Emmy, whose distress was obvious. Whatever did Judith mean? And then the penny dropped. It was not Carew she was speaking of but Rees, Rees whom Emmy loved, Rees who had eyes for no one . . . but me? I was horrified. Could it be true? I had never thought of such a thing.

I had known for some time of Emmy's feelings, and I thought that she and Rees were courting as they say in the country, and that it was the same between them as between Carew and myself. It had never entered my head that Rees did not care for Emmy, and that this should be because of me was inconceivable.

An uneasy silence had fallen with Judith's words, a silence of shock, of embarrassment, and I plunged in with silly prattle to relieve the tension.

"Catch, Carew!" I cried, picking up the topmost apple and tossing it to him. "Taste it and see if it is bitter or sweet."

He caught it deftly and bit into it, making a wry face as he did so.

"Bitter," he said, "bitter." And he turned and deliberately rolled the apple across the floor to Judith's feet.

Hastily I began to peel another, and Emmy to work her pastry as if her life depended on it.

My father called from the hall. "Fetch up a jug of cider from the cellar, Carew, like a good fellow." And Judith rose to her feet and walked out of the kitchen, her eyes stony.

"How could she?" I said to Carew later. "It was a beastly thing to say, a thing she knew would hurt you and me, but Emmy most of all."

"It's true, you know," said Carew gently. "Rees worships you, I've noticed him watching you. Still that does not mean that he won't marry Emmy and live happily ever after."

"Marry Emmy when he does not love her!" I exclaimed.

"Yes, it has been done you know. Don't take it too much to heart, Liss. He'll get over it."

But I did take it to heart, and after Carew had gone I sat at the window of my bedroom in the darkness, wondering what to do.

I could have a blazing row with Judith and tell her what I thought of her. But what would be the use? It would not help Emmy Lee.

I could suggest that Emmy leave us and get work somewhere else; go back to London perhaps, for a while. But I knew that her home was with us and she would never be happy away from us.

I could creep into her room now and, under the kindly cover of darkness, talk with her and ease my mind. But in the end I did none of these things. The situation was too delicate a one to talk about, and I decided that it was kinder to say nothing. So I went to bed.

Early the next morning Judith departed, and I was glad to see her go. Although I was ashamed of my feelings, in my inmost heart I hoped that she would make her life abroad and never return to disturb the peace of our life in the Old Court.

A week later Emmy had a letter from an elderly friend in London with whom she had kept in touch, a housekeeper to an eccentric old gentleman. This woman wrote to say that her employer was going away for two weeks and asked Emmy to come and keep her company in the house.

Emmy Lee showed me the letter, which she did not take seriously at all.

"As if I could walk out from here any moment I like!" she exclaimed.

"But Emmy, wouldn't you like to go?" I asked. "You haven't had a proper holiday since we came to Wales, and this seems a wonderful chance to have one. It could easily be arranged, you know."

At first, Emmy shook her head and would not consider the suggestion, but after a while, she changed her mind. I persuaded her to let me ask my mother about it, and she agreed that of course Emmy must go. Emmy wrote back accepting the invitation with enthusiasm.

I took her into our nearest town and helped her choose a coat and dress and a new hat.

It was arranged that I should take over the cooking, with Mrs. Owen to help me, during Emmy's absence, and it was with a light heart that I accompanied her to the station on a crisp October morning a few days later. Young Rees drove us in the six miles by the shore road, and several times I saw him turn and stare at Emmy as if he had never noticed her before. She looked charming in her new clothes, her face rosy with excitement.

"Perhaps you'll enjoy London so much that you'll want to stay there, Emmy," I said, teasingly, although there was a serious intention behind my words.

"There's no saying, Miss Liss. I might indeed." She answered me lightly, in the same tone as I had used, and I noticed Rees glance sharply at her to see if she was in earnest. She took my hand in hers and squeezed it, belying her words. I knew she would never leave us, dear Emmy Lee.

"Have a wonderful holiday," I called, as the train puffed importantly out of the tiny station.

She stretched towards me out of the carriage window, as if loath to leave me, fearful of removing from me the shelter of her protective love.

Rees was waiting for me by the dogcart in the station yard, and I had one or two purchases to make for my mother, and a carpenter to collect who was coming to us for the day to carry out various repairs.

The house felt empty at first with Emmy gone, and I realized how much I depended on her companionship when Briony and Carew were absent. My mother was now suffering from more frequent attacks of asthma, during which she retired to bed and liked to keep very quiet till she was better. My father was not with her so much, as his work took him farther afield each year as his good reputation became known.

I got on well with Mrs. Owen, but it was very hard to get to know her properly, and although I saw a good deal of her while she was working in the house during Emmy's absence, I found her very shy now that I was no longer a child.

She would talk about her wild creatures and allow me to help her with the casualties she treated—a broken wing, or a foot caught in a trap—and she told me a lot about the habits of her favorites, the seals; but when I talked about her, she became embarrassed and shut herself away from my chatter. I hoped she might have taken me to Seal Cove to watch the seals coming to her call, for I had not forgotten what her son had told us about her strange power with them, nor the seal song Briony and I had heard coming from her cottage. But although I showed my interest in the seals, she never asked me to come to Seal Cove with her, and I did not like to ask her to take me unless she suggested it herself.

# CHAPTER SEVEN

I THINK IT WAS A FEW NIGHTS BEFORE EMMY'S RETURN from her holiday that we had the first fierce storm of that winter. The shrieking wind tore round the house, rattling windows and doors and shaking the whole structure with its violent onslaught. Great sheets of rain beat against the windows, battering the walls, flattening the flowers in the garden and the grass in the fields around. The trees moaned and creaked, flung and tortured by the gale, and I was glad that the old weeping ash stood protected in the shelter of the house.

The storm was over next morning and a tremulous sun came out. Soon the rain-washed sky was blue and cloudless again. The whole countryside lay sunnily, deceptively, peaceful after the night of violence, like a child spent with a storm of tears. After tea I put on my heavy shoes and went outside. The house was deserted, my father at his surgery in the village and my mother at one of her women's meetings in the church.

Mrs. Owen would soon be coming in to cook our supper so I left the back door open. I did not intend to go far, but my feet turned of their own accord on to the field path that led to the sea, and I found myself following it towards Seal Cove.

There were signs all round me of the previous night's gale: roofs torn off barns, trees uprooted, paths turned into stony torrents down which the rain water had escaped to the sea. The fields were drenched and shining with moisture, a steady steam rose from them as they dried in the late sunshine. All this should have been warning enough to me that the storm had left its mark. But unheeding and with no thought of danger, I came to the edge of the cliff above Seal Cove and peered down. Far below me on the ledge by the sea, sat Rees fishing, probably for our supper. I had not even time to call out to him before the ghastly thing happened. One moment I stood poised on the edge, the next I felt earth begin to crumble and slide under my feet and a chunk of the cliff, loosened by the storm, broke away, carrying me, helpless with it.

I felt myself plunging through the air towards the rocks and the hungry sea below. I remember my utter horror and despair, trying to scream and, as in a nightmare, finding that I could not. It was all over in a moment—I dropped into blackness. . . .

I think the shock of the icy water must have brought me to my senses, for I found myself half drowned but lying on rock, and heard the sobbing of a young man's voice in my ears.

"Oh, Miss, my dear Miss. Open your eyes. Show me you are alive." It was Rees's voice, and I was thankful to know that he was with me before I slipped down into the blackness again.

The next time I came round I was being carried and there were muffled voices and dim shapes and a blessed numbness, due no doubt to the injection that must have been given me.

Then I found myself in bed and my father repeating, "Swallow it, Melissa, there's a good girl, just swallow it." I don't know what "it" was, but I did my best to obey him.

There followed days of semi-consciousness when a nurse hovered around me, and I lost all sense of time. People and voices came and went as I struggled slowly back to life.

In some miraculous way I had escaped being battered to death on the rocks of Seal Cove. I had fallen into deep water, and Rees had managed to get me ashore, thus saving my life.

I was less gravely hurt than had at first been feared, they said. I was badly shocked and bruised, and my muscles were painfully torn, but nothing seemed to have been broken or irreparably damaged. Yet the days went by and I was absolutely unable to move my legs; they were paralyzed, helpless. And over and over again in my mind I did that ghastly terrifying rush downwards through the air into the hungry sea.

A London specialist, an old friend of my father's, was called in.

"You must be patient," he told me. "You are still suffering from shock. I can find no permanent damage to the spine or legs, but you have had a very bad fright which may take you some time to get over, and this paralysis is nature's way of keeping you quiet. I do assure you that there is nothing to prevent your getting on to your feet again as soon as you are ready to make the effort. You are very lucky to be alive, young lady!"

Carew rushed down from Oxford to see me, and his presence did more to cheer me than anything else could have done. Everyone was very kind, efficient, and helpful, and the doctors kept assuring me it was only a matter of time, but each day my heart sank a little lower —time can be forever.

After a month or so the nurse departed, and Emmy Lee, who was very strong, took over the care of me at her own request. But there were days when I was suddenly seized by bouts of acute pain and I could not bear even Emmy Lee to touch me. Then I sent for Mrs. Owen, for I remembered how Young Rees had spoken of her gentle hand. Indeed I had seen it when she worked with her sick animals, and now I knew her soothing power for myself. Doctors came again and clustered round my bed, even the one from London.

"This pain you complain of," he said. "Tell me about it. What kind of pain is it?"

"Very bad, when it comes," I answered. "Like red hot pins and needles, or terrible growing pains in my back and legs."

He looked thoughtful and a little puzzled, and he asked me more questions. Then he said a very strange thing. "Are you sure it is *real* pain you suffer, not *imagined* pain?" I looked at him in utter astonishment.

"What ever do you mean?" I cried. "It is very real to me." He turned away from me and I heard him mutter something about "hysteria; psychological shock," which didn't seem to me to make any sense.

The days dragged on through the misty tang of early winter and, when I could not sleep, I lay at night watching the stars in the frosty sky, wondering what was to become of me.

I had been given the old study on the ground floor, but I longed for my white room at the top of the house, my own place.

Then Briony came home and it was Christmas time, and Carew hung about despondent till I persuaded him to rejoin the winter sports party he had given up for my sake. Once he was gone, I began to play a game with myself. "By the time he comes back, I'll be able to wiggle my toes again," or, "By the time he comes I'll be able to bend one knee." But day succeeded day, and even with massage and treatment there was no improvement in my dead limbs; and slowly, slowly, I drove myself to face the awful possibility that I might never walk again.

Fear hung like a black cloud over me, threatening, menacing. What if I should lose Carew?

Gradually the leaden days lengthened into spring. I could hear the cries of the new lambs in the fields, and the lovely wild call of the curlew mocked me from the moor where Carew and I had wandered, enraptured, only a few months earlier.

One of my mother's friends interested me in tapestry, and I spent long hours cross-stitching, in varicolored wools, designs for chair seats. I did not enjoy this work, but I was grateful to the kind woman for teaching me, it helped to pass the time.

One day, a splendid wheel chair arrived, and I was lifted into it and pushed outside into the fresh air. Soon I could manage the chair myself, and my father had a ramp built from the side door of the house into the garden.

He also bought me a handsome dog, a red setter. I called him Sergeant, and he became my devoted companion and attendant. He was always with me and slept across my door at night.

Everyone remarked on how well I looked and how wonderful it was to see me getting about again. It was wonderful, but my legs remained utterly useless and I wondered more than ever if I was to remain a cripple for the rest of my life.

My parents tried everything they could think of. New doctors gave their opinions, new treatments were devised. But still nothing happened; I could not move my legs.

Mrs. Owen and Emmy Lee nursed me devotedly, lifting me and caring for me; never had anyone better or kinder friends. Sometimes Mrs. Owen would push my chair through our orchard and along the field path to her cottage. She would allow me to handle her injured creatures, and this gave me great pleasure.

Suddenly it was June. Carew, now twenty-one, had done his finals and come down from Oxford, and Judith arrived home from abroad. Immediately she took possession of my room on the top floor—she had always liked it better than her own, she said.

She was exquisite, irresistible, and she knew it; but I understood what lay behind the lovely mask—a deadly selfishness, an implacable will, and I saw in her eyes a look of secret triumph that froze my heart—Judith had not changed.

The words Carew had once said of her burned in my mind: *I'm afraid she'll compel me to do something against my will, something devilish, something she wants.*

The fear that had hung over me for months slowly crystallized, and I saw clearly my danger. But I was helpless, my recovery was uncertain, my confidence gone. I was crippled in body and despairing in mind. I could not fight her beauty and her power.

And my forebodings were fully justified, for before the summer was over, Carew and Judith ran away together and were married in London.

PART II  *DILYS*

# CHAPTER ONE

I THINK I WAS ONLY SIX YEARS OLD WHEN I FIRST AC-
knowledged to myself that my mother did not love me.
I had been to a children's party, escorted, there and back,
in the pony trap by Young Rees. We had the hood up
because of the cold, and I was tucked in beside him with
rugs and shawls and a hot water bottle.

Aunt Liss's beautiful dog Sergeant had come to the
door with Emmy Lee to see me off, but even the temptation of a run with his friend, Betsy the pony, could not
lure him from his mistress's side on a gray day when she
had to stay indoors.

I felt a little sick as we clopped along the deserted

country road, and I shivered inside my thick cloak with the nervous anticipation of a child going to its first party.

Emmy Lee had wanted to come with me, but I had refused her offer—if my mother would not come with me, I must go alone, for I knew that other mothers would be there with their children.

I pulled my shawl closer round my head and addressed myself to Rees, who was a very silent person of whom I was a little afraid—I always felt he disapproved of me for some reason.

"Where is Grandfather today?" I asked.

"Gone to town to a conference of doctors," he replied shortly.

"He must be very old to be a doctor still," I remarked. Rees chuckled.

"Not so old as you'd think, Missie," he grunted. "Though I will say he has aged a lot since your grandmother died."

"I don't remember my grandmother. Was she like Aunt Liss?"

The moment I mentioned Aunt Liss his manner warmed to me.

"No, no," he said. "There's no one like Miss Liss. Your Aunt Briony is more like your grandmother."

"Aunt Briony lives in Canada and I've never seen her," I remarked. "Aunt Liss made my party frock," I confided. "It is white silk, smocked in pink, and I have a pink sash and a pink band on my hair."

"Indeed now," said Rees smiling. "You must look very nice under all your shawls."

Soon we turned up a long drive and came to the big gray house where the party was to be given. Rees lifted me down and saw me into the lighted hall. There I was seized upon by a young maid in a black dress and a stiff white muslin cap and apron, who bustled me upstairs and proceeded to help me off with my bundles of outdoor clothes. She helped me to change into my silk socks and my new pink dancing shoes, and she brushed my hair, and admired my dress, and took me downstairs to an enormous room thronged with children. I found myself shaking hands with a tall lady, whom I had met before, the mother of the Thomas children who sometimes came to tea with me at the Old Court. It was their party.

"How are you, Dilys, my dear," said the lady. "I'm sorry your mother could not come too. Now let me see —Marion, here is Dilys. Come and look after her," and she dismissed me with a quick smile.

"You're not nearly so beautiful as *my* mother," I said to myself, as cozy plump Marion took my hand and led me into the jostling throng.

We played with balloons and I had a gorgeous flame-colored one, which touched a sprig of holly and burst. I managed to get into a corner by myself, and no one noticed till I had finished crying; and then it was time for tea.

We were all seated round an enormous table and there were more lovely things to eat than I had ever seen.

A lot of mothers sat round the fire at one end of the room, and kept coming along to see how their children were getting on.

On one side of me there was a quiet little girl whose
nannie stood beside her, and was nice to me too. I found
that I was much too excited to eat, and although there
were at least six kinds of sandwiches, and scones and
drop scones, and brandy snaps filled with cream, and
iced cakes and meringues and jellies in little dishes, I
found I could not swallow more than one drop scone—
they were not so good as the ones Emmy Lee made—and
one of my favorite meringues. The boy sitting next to
me never spoke a word, just ate and ate and ate. He grew
redder and redder in the face till at last he whispered, "If
I eat another thing I shall burst." At that moment somebody pulled a cracker and I thought he had.

After tea there was a magic lantern and pictures of
funny men called clowns behaving very badly. Most of
the children sat on their mother's knees to watch, snug-
gling against them, happy and safe. I liked watching them
better than the magic lantern. Gradually it dawned on
me that this was something I was missing. I never sat
on my mother's knee or felt her arms around me. There
was no love between us, she could not be bothered with
me. On my side there was a shy adoration, but on hers,
nothing, no gentleness, no comfort, only a cold remote-
ness, and a beauty that made my heart ache.

Just before the lantern slides came to an end, while I
was still absorbed in my study of the other children, I
heard one mother whisper to another.

"Who is the little girl with the lost look?"

"The Grenville child, my dear. Judith's daughter,"
replied the other. "What a house for a child to grow up

in. Poor sweet Melissa, and that hateful Judith! They say she is quite mad, and never goes out."

I felt a flicker of anger begin to rise from my toes and flame right through my whole body to my face, and I turned my head away so that they would not see that I had heard them.

They were speaking of my mother. How *dared* they say such horrible things about her. Cruel wicked things. I began to tremble, and in one more minute would have exploded into a frightful scene, but a storm of clapping and shouting broke out, applause for the lantern slides, which had come to an end.

Then, oh then, a wonderful thing happened.

Into the room two servants pushed a large barrel organ on wheels, and one of them began to turn its handle and to grind out a gay catchy tune.

Mothers and children crowded round it, shouting excitedly.

"Where did it come from?"

"Who found it?"

"What a tremendous joke!"

"Humphrey found it in London and bought it for an old song," said someone.

But I had no ears for their chatter. My entire being was entranced by the lilting rhythm of that garish music. A tumult of excitement burst in me. My toes began to tingle. My body rose light as air, and forgetting entirely where I was, who I was, I surrendered myself to the spell of the music and began to dance.

Round and round that great room I danced, with joy

and abandon, oblivious of everything but the wild music
and the magic in my feet. I was unaware of the astonished silence that had fallen on the company till as if in
a dream I heard someone say, "Who is she?"

"Isn't it the little Grenville girl? Where did she learn
to dance?"

Enraptured, I danced on and on.

At last the music stopped, and I sank down onto the
nearest chair. For a moment there was silence, then a
great burst of applause greeted me, and children and their
mothers crowded round me.

"Bravo, Dilly!" said my hostess. "That was splendid.
I had no idea you could dance so well!"

Neither had I until I responded to the music.

After a pause the tune started up again, and the boy
who sat next to me at tea sidled up to me.

"I saw you dancing," he said. "I'd like to dance with
you, but . . . I wish I hadn't eaten so much!"

I sat there happily, watching the other children ga-
lumphing round the room, but I did not launch myself
again on that bewitching tide of music. I was replete and
satisfied, and I felt compensated for some of the less
happy moments of that bewildering afternoon.

I rode home with Rees, in my warm cocoon of shawls
and wraps, through a flurry of snow to Emmy Lee who
awaited me in the lighted doorway. Rees carried me into
the warm kitchen and deposited me by the stove, and
Emmy began to peel off my outer garments.

"How did you get on, dearie? Was it lovely? Did you
have a happy time?" she asked.

"It was wonderful, Emmy, it was gorgeous! There was a barrel organ—and I danced."

"Did you now!" cried Emmy Lee. "But what a funny thing to have at a children's party, a barrel organ? Are you sure?"

"Yes, yes!" I shouted rapturously. "You couldn't help dancing to it. Look, I'll show you." And I jumped to my feet and began to skip and twirl around the kitchen.

"Well!" exclaimed Emmy Lee admiringly when I had finished. "It's like having a fairy in the kitchen. Come and have your supper now, dearie, and tell me some more."

She sat me up at the kitchen table and ladled out a mug of delicious-smelling soup, which she set before me with a chunk of her homemade bread, and I discovered I was very hungry. While she chopped vegetables for the grownups' dinner, I told her about the party, the sumptuous tea, the magic lantern, the shouting gleeful crowd of children, the watching mothers; but then I fell silent remembering my discovery.

"Some mothers call their children 'darling,'" I remarked, half to myself.

Emmy Lee looked at me and put down the vegetable knife on the table, and she picked me up in her arms.

"There's my dearie, my pet," she said. "Come and tell Aunt Liss about the party before I put you to bed."

Aunt Liss sat in her wheel chair, her head bent over her embroidery. Her face was shadowed and withdrawn till she saw me. Sergeant lay at her feet, and on the other side of the fireplace my grandfather nodded over an open book. My mother was not there.

Suddenly I felt exhausted; my excitement had faded, and I wanted to go to bed.

"You must see her dance, Miss Liss," said Emmy Lee. "I'd never have believed it. She dances like a gypsy, like a flame."

"Tomorrow you'll dance for me, Dilly, won't you?" said Aunt Liss gently as I kissed her good night, and Emmy Lee tiptoed out of the room with me so as not to waken grandfather.

"Where's mother?" I asked warily. "Can I say good night to her?"

"Better not disturb her," Emmy answered promptly. "She's in her room with one of her headaches."

But Emmy Lee made a pursed mouth. She was full of disapproval, not sympathy.

As soon as I had snuggled down between my warm smooth sheets, and Emmy had tucked me up and kissed me good night, leaving the door propped half open so that a fan of light filtered into the shadowy room, I expected to fall asleep at once, but I could not.

Images chased one another round my mind, snatches of conversation, memories of laughter, all the gay kaleidoscope of that exciting afternoon; but for me, at the heart of it all, there was a sadness, an emptiness which swelled and rose like a bubble till it burst into my conscious mind. I sat up in bed, and the words tumbled out of my mouth.

"My mother does not love me."

I must have sat hunched up there in the darkness for quite some time thinking things out; I had never asked questions up till then; it was time I began. I knew very little about myself, about my father and my strange mother, about the uncomfortable atmosphere in the house, which even I could sense everywhere, except in the kitchen, and there lay peace, my security, my safety, with Emmy Lee.

"Emmy Lee"—I repeated her name aloud and found comfort in the sound. She was the one to question about all those uncomfortable things that puzzled me. Aunt Liss must not be distressed by them. That settled, quickly I fell asleep.

# CHAPTER TWO

THAT CHILDREN'S PARTY WAS OF FAR-REACHING IMPORtance to me, a turning point in my life. Apparently my impromptu dancing performance had caused quite a stir, and for a week or two after the party there were callers at the Old Court. Since my mother had gone to London, they saw Aunt Liss. I was invited into the drawing room, and Aunt Liss asked me to show what I could do. But the flame was not in me, I needed the tinder of exciting music to set me alight; my feet felt heavy as stone; I could not show off. Aunt Liss was disappointed I could see, and thought I was overcome with shyness. But on one occasion, Mrs. Glynn-Thomas, who had given the party, was there and seemed to have an inkling of my difficulties. She became my champion.

"Shall we have some music?" she suggested, and she sat down at our neglected piano and began to play a Chopin mazurka. The wild music filled the sedate room. I felt my toes begin to tingle, and a lightness and fire filled my whole body. I forgot my audience of watching ladies, my restricted surroundings, my dislike of "showing off," and almost of their own accord my feet took me onto the polished floor; I abandoned myself to the magic of the glorious music and began to dance. Chairs and rugs were pushed out of my way as I whirled like a leaf before the wind.

At last the music stopped. There was a murmur of voices and well-bred clapping. The tumult in my blood subsided, leaving me glowing from crown to toe, and I sank down beside Aunt Liss's chair, suddenly horribly selfconscious.

"You see, don't you?" said Mrs. Glynn-Thomas crossing to us. "The child must have dancing lessons—ballet. She has the makings of a dancer. Even now, young and untrained, she is a delight to watch."

I glanced up at Aunt Liss to see if she agreed and noticed with astonishment that her eyes were filled with tears.

That was the beginning of my dancing career, for the following week I started ballroom dancing at a class given once a week in a tall house near Newcove. Our teacher was Swedish. We called her Miss Clara. She was plain and proper and looked as if she had swallowed a poker and was unable to bend. But her young assistant, Miss Julie, with her gay sparkling smile, I loved at first sight. She was dark and rosy-cheeked and danced with a lissome grace as if she enjoyed it.

At first I was sick every Wednesday with sheer excitement, so that I missed several classes; but gradually I learned to quiet my feelings a little, and I soon found that I far outstripped the rest of the class. The dancing was dull, restricted, too well-bred, and above all too easy. At least these classes enabled me to plead for a gramophone and records so that I might practice my steps at home. But the dancing I practiced was of my own composition when my flying feet carried me into an exciting world of fantasy.

Soon Miss Julie came to my rescue and asked to see my mother who, as so often happened, was out when she arrived; so she saw Aunt Liss instead.

"She has remarkable talent. I would like to give her private ballet lessons," I overheard Miss Julie say as I helped Emmy Lee carry in the tea. "Later she should go to London and learn at a school of ballet."

My heart soared with joy, then bounced as I wondered what my mother would have to say. But I need not have worried. My mother was not sufficiently interested in me or my future to be bothered about it, and it was left for Aunt Liss to arrange my classes with Miss Julie. She came three times a week and taught me in the drawing room. I discovered in myself a demon for work, when the work was dancing.

Then the matter of my schooling had to be settled,

and it was decided that Aunt Liss should give me lessons every morning; so my life took on a certain pattern and routine.

About this time I began to ask those questions about the things in my life that had puzzled me ever since the party. I questioned Emmy Lee about my father. Why did no one ever mention him, and how had he died? Why did my mother and Aunt Liss dislike one another? Why did my mother behave so strangely, and why did she never take me with her when she went on her frequent visits to London?

Emmy Lee gave me the bare bones of the knowledge I wanted, but later on I had to clothe them myself with the little snippets of information picked up here and there and carefully pieced together over a number of years. From Emmy I learned that my parents had sailed for India as soon as they were married.

"They cut themselves off from us," said Emmy, "and we didn't have many letters. The war made it difficult, of course, and they couldn't get home even if they'd wanted to. It's a pity you never knew your father," she went on. "He was such a gentle young man. Things might have been very different for you if he had lived, if he had not been killed in battle just before you were born."

"No one tells me about him," I complained. "My mother never speaks of him. Perhaps she misses him so much that it makes her sad to talk about him."

Emmy Lee snorted and her black eyes flashed brightly.

"Very likely," she snapped. "Very likely." But I

knew from the way she said it that it wasn't what she meant at all.

"You'd better ask your Aunt Liss about him," she said at last. "She's the one to tell you."

"Oh, did she know him very well?" I asked. "I thought Aunt Liss and Mother . . . well, they don't seem to be very good friends."

"Small wonder!" exclaimed Emmy Lee, and her mouth snapped shut like a purse, so I knew it was no use asking any more just then.

It was after she had begun to give me lessons that I got to know Aunt Liss as a person. Up till then she had been my dearly loved aunt, but a cripple and an invalid, and not quite real. Now I began to probe under this picture I had of her to discover the real person.

The discovery started one day when we were having a French lesson in the garden.

Sergeant lay by Aunt Liss's wheel chair, and I sat beside her under the twisted old ash tree.

"I can climb as far as the first hole in the trunk," I said proudly, pointing above me. "I did it yesterday."

"Well done," said Aunt Liss. "Next you must climb to the top where my tree house used to be."

"Your tree house!" I exclaimed in astonishment. "You used to climb that tree? But I thought . . . I did not know . . . ." I faltered fearing to hurt her. "I did not know that you had proper legs."

Aunt Liss burst into a peal of laughter and pulled off the light rug she always wore tucked across her knees.

"Look!" she cried. "Feel them. They're quite real,

you see, though useless now. I had an accident, Dilly, nearly ten years ago," and she told me the dreadful story of how she had fallen down the cliff into the sea.

I listened, horrified, till she had finished.

"But your legs look all right," I cried, "and you're quite young really. Surely you'll be able to walk again someday?"

She shook her head. "I've given up trying," she said sadly. "It doesn't matter any more."

Sergeant rose and put his nose into her hand comfortingly. I puzzled and puzzled over what she could mean. Why did it not matter any more? Why had she given up trying? It was quite beyond my understanding. However from that day I became deeply interested in her. My whole attitude towards her changed. It was then that I began to put her in my mother's place, and gradually she became to me everything that I would have liked my mother to be.

Often after we had finished my lessons, I would ask Aunt Liss to tell me about my father, and she would recall some little incident, or repeat some story about him so intimately and lovingly that I soon began to feel that I knew him myself.

One day I said to her, "You must have known him very well to remember him so clearly—I think you were very fond of him."

Aunt Liss blushed and then went pale. "He was a very special person to me," she said quietly.

I saw less and less of my mother. She seemed more and more to shut herself up in her studio at the top of

the house, painting I suppose. Sometimes she went out
striding over the rough heathery hills, and came in
soaked and exhausted; or else she was away in London.
I had accepted the bitter fact that she did not care for
me, but this did not prevent me from hoping that one
day her feelings for me would change. The more she
kept herself aloof from me, the more I craved to be
with her and resented her frequent absences.

Then one night a horrible thing happened to me.

My mother had been away for more than two weeks
on one of her visits to London, and was to return the
next day.

I went to bed in my little room next to Emmy Lee,
full of joyful anticipation, planning how I would welcome my mother, and how this time everything would
be different and she would be overjoyed to see me.

I woke in the dark, struggling for breath, as if a great
weight lay on my chest, choking the life out of me. I
sat up in a panic, wheezing and gasping, sweating with
fear. Whatever had happened to me? I must be ill. My
heart thudded, and I shuddered with terror as I fought
for each difficult breath. I crawled out of bed, not even
waiting to light my candle, and stumbled, coughing and
choking, along the passage to Emmy Lee's room, gasping out, "Emmy, Emmy, I think I'm going to die."

Emmy Lee was wide awake in a second and gathered
me into her warm bed, comforting and soothing me. "It's
only a touch of asthma, my dearie," she declared, holding
me close in her arms. "It will pass, you'll see. Your
granny used to get it. There's nothing to worry about.

Just stop fretting now, and I'll fetch you a hot drink in a minute and you'll go to sleep again and wake up perfectly all right in the morning."

I could not believe her, but the comfort of her presence as much as her words reassured me. The horrible choking nightmare receded a little, and my breathing became slightly less difficult. Soon she was able to leave me propped up in her bed, with a sturdy candle for company, while she went to light the spirit lamp under the kettle to make me a hot drink. She knew exactly what to do, and later on I realized that she must have had the same experience with my grandmother on many occasions. What she put into my cup I do not know, but it tasted nasty. Gradually the load lifted from my chest enabling me to breathe more slowly and evenly, and soon I fell into a sleep of exhaustion.

In the morning I woke late, but the nightmare attack was over, leaving me limp but normal. My mother returned in the afternoon. She was cold and beautiful as usual. There was no love in her chill greeting; she was not glad to see me; the miracle had not happened, and once again my hopes collapsed.

But the nightmare attacks of asthma became a recurring horror. Always before my mother returned to the Old Court, or at times when I was worried or anxious, they came to plague me.

# CHAPTER THREE

A CHILD ACCEPTS A GREAT DEAL IN ITS LIFE THAT A grownup would question, and if my mother lived in a peculiar way, I accepted it as natural to her and thought little of it. In any case she was an artist, and everyone knows that artists can be as queer as they please.

Much of her time, when she was at home, was spent in her studio, as I have said, drawing and painting; but nobody was allowed to see her work, and I was never permitted to enter the studio. Only once, in the garden, I came on her suddenly from behind, and she did not hear me, so that I was able to stand and stare at her almost finished picture. It was a full length portrait of a foreign-looking lady dressed in rich clothes of brilliant colors, her black hair piled high on her proud head. The face was arresting, imperious, disdainful, and something else—wicked. The eyes slanted slightly, and the complexion was very smooth and faintly yellow, the color of a tea rose.

It was a fascinating face, but malevolent. The whole vivid picture sent a cold shiver down my back, and I turned and retreated before my mother even knew that I had been there.

A few days later a peculiar thing happened. I had gone to fetch something for Emmy Lee from her bedroom. I think she was doing some sewing for my mother, who was leaving the next day on one of her visits to London.

I crossed to the window and knelt by it for a minute, gazing out onto the newly unfolded leaves of the great weeping ash, and there, climbing down the tree I saw my mother. As I watched, she glanced around her to make sure she was unobserved, then she swung herself lightly to the ground, ran across the grass, and disappeared into the house through the front door below me.

I was used to my mother behaving differently from other people, but this seemed a very strange thing for even her to do. Grownups did not climb trees, and she had looked furtive. What had she been doing? Hiding something? In that hole in the tree trunk? I knew all about the hole, for I had thought of hiding something there myself.

Next morning as soon as she was gone, I climbed the

tree to investigate, put my hand tentatively into the hole and felt something hard and smooth. Gently I pulled it out. It was a package tied up in oilskin.

I undid the string and carefully took off the outer covering. Next there was a piece of white linen, and when I had unrolled that I found inside it a slim wooden doll, beautifully dressed in red velvet. I was excited and astonished not only by the strange circumstances, but also because I recognized the doll. I knew that smooth polished face with the slanting eyes—it was the fascinating, wicked face of the lady in the picture I had seen my mother painting. I stared at her for several minutes, holding her in my hands, while my dislike and anger mounted. Then hastily I wrapped her up again and pushed her back into the hole. I wanted to have nothing to do with her; she was repulsive, and I hated her.

How could my mother cherish this horrible creature? And why had she hidden her in the tree?

I puzzled over my discovery for a long time. The only solution I could think of was that my mother still loved her old doll; but because she was grownup, she was ashamed of her childish feelings, so she had hidden the doll in that most secret place, the hole in the tree.

I told no one about it, not Aunt Liss not Emmy Lee; but soon after my mother's return home when I climbed to the hole and felt inside, it was empty. The doll was gone.

One day, a month or two later, I found in a magazine an article about my mother's work, and several reproductions of her pictures, mostly portraits. That same

strange inimical face appeared in every one of them.

"Great curiosity has been aroused in those who admire Judith Mansell's work, as to the identity of her model. Who is this distinguished unusual looking woman?" asked the writer of the article.

I could have told them whose was the mysterious face. How astonished they would have been to learn that the unknown model, the proud great lady, was nothing but an old wooden doll.

The long days of childhood passed slowly, and I was content with my lessons with Aunt Liss, my dancing classes with Miss Julie, and my occasional expeditions into the outside world, escorted by Young Rees. I spent a lot of time reading, for through books I could escape into a rich world of fantasy and adventure.

My grandfather became, suddenly, a fretful invalid as the result of a stroke, and before long he had to be moved to a nursing home where I sometimes used to visit him with Emmy Lee.

It was after his death that the decision was made that I was to go to boarding school in London, where I could join a ballet class and have real ballet lessons. I hated leaving Aunt Liss and Emmy Lee and Rees and the Old Court; but as I grew older I had become more aware of the tension between Aunt Liss and my mother, and I felt relieved to be escaping from this shadow in the house.

I had never been able to discover what lay at the root of their enmity, and Emmy Lee would not tell me; but I knew that there was deep-seated and bitter distrust between them, and I was convinced that it had something to do with me.

Then one evening just after my twelfth birthday, a few weeks before I was to leave for school, I stumbled on their painful secret.

I had gone to see Mrs. Owen in her cottage on the edge of the moor. I loved helping her with her tame creatures and listening to her stories about the seals, and helping her to get tea ready for Young Rees when he came in from work. Often I brought a book with me and lay flat on the heather reading or dreaming, for this was the kingdom of the curlews, and I loved to listen to their haunting cries.

On this particular evening I helped her as much as I could, breaking the sticks for her fire, bringing in her washing from the line, and setting the table for Rees's supper. It was one of her bad days when her poor legs were full of aches and pains, and she was compelled to keep to the house.

When all was ready and we were waiting for Rees to come, I knelt by the open window, gazing up the little valley, or Cwm as they call it in Wales, to the heathery hills beyond.

"This is one of the places I shall miss most when I am in London," I said. "This little Cwm and the curlews. There must be magic here."

"Aye, the magic of joy and of sorrow. You are not the first to know it," said Mrs. Owen nodding her head, "nor the first to love that place neither. They used to come down from it, their eyes shining like stars, their feet light on the ground, treading on dreams."

"They?" I asked. "Who are they?"

"Why your father and *her* of course," Mrs. Owen answered tartly as if I ought to have known. "Walking in a fairyland of their own, they were. Many a time I seen them, she with her gentle face glowing with happiness and no thought of disaster. Aye me! Aye me!" She rocked herself backwards and forwards crooning tunelessly while I tried to sort out what she had said. So my mother had been different when she was young—happy and gentle; it must have been the disaster of my father's death that had changed her so much. But why did Mrs. Owen, who spoke of her so lovingly, never see her now? My mother never came near her cottage, of that I was certain. Had they quarreled? When Mrs. Owen came to the house, it was always Aunt Liss she came to see.

But I was glad to think that my parents had been happy together when they were young. Perhaps some day I would find that gentleness in my mother again.

"Did my mother and father come to see you?" I asked.

Mrs. Owen's crooning stopped and she looked at me, first in astonishment and then in fury.

"Your mother?" She almost spat the words at me. "Your mother never came here."

"But you said she and my father came often to this place . . ."

"Not your mother, never that one!" cried Mrs. Owen violently. "Miss Liss, my Miss Liss and your father, o'course. It was *her* your father loved, not . . . that other

one. The wicked one! The cruel! Stole him from my
Miss Liss she did. Saw her chance and took it after the
accident happened. Put a spell on him, she did, and
swept the silly young man off his feet, and all for spite,
for *spite*. She never cared for him, nor for anyone; not
she . . . not . . . that one."

Mrs Owen's spurt of rage flickered out, and she began to mumble and mutter to herself, oblivious of me,
while I stood rooted to the floor, staring at her in horrified amazement.

Did she know what she had said? Could I believe her?
Could there be any truth in her story? Or was it all in
the imagination of a foolish old woman?

If it had really been Aunt Liss my father had loved,
why had he not married her? Couldn't he have waited
for her a year, two years, till she had recovered? Surely
she *could* have got better just to marry him? Or had it
been hopeless from the start? Had my mother taken pity
on the poor young man, so devastated by the twist his
fate had taken? Perhaps Aunt Liss had refused to marry
him because of her injury and my mother had hoped to
comfort and console him, knowing Aunt Liss would
never walk again? Perhaps my mother had really loved
him. Perhaps she was a kind person after all?

I wished I could believe this was true, but I knew in
my heart it was not. I could not forget how often my
mother had humiliated and rebuffed me, the countless
times I had fled from her biting tongue to Emmy Lee
for comfort. I had never seen pity in my mother's hard
eyes, nor gentleness nor compassion. I feared she was

incapable of loving anyone; and who should know it
better than I, her child?

But what of Aunt Liss herself? She remembered my
father with love; she bore him no resentment. Surely
he could not have deserted her in her helplessness after
her accident? It was unthinkable. Yet there must have
been some reason for his behavior, some irresistible
power that he could not withstand.

I found myself beginning to tremble. I must find out
the truth. It could not be worse than my imaginings.

Mrs. Owen did not notice when I left her to her
twilight world and slipped out of her cottage. I ran
along the path to the orchard, making for the warm
shelter of our kitchen, and Emmy Lee.

The savory smell of liver and bacon met me at the
door as I rushed in and threw myself at Emmy, who
stood by the stove chopping onions.

"Emmy, Emmy! I know now," I cried. "I *know* about
Aunt Liss and my father!" And I burst into the most

painful and violent sobbing.

"Hush, hush. Whoever has been telling you those old tales?" Emmy asked in a shocked voice. "That crazy old woman, Mrs. Owen, I suppose. She doesn't know what she's saying half the time. She shouldn't have told you, dearie." She held me tightly in her safe strong arms, and soon I was able to calm myself and stop crying.

"You must tell me *all* of it," I begged. "I can trust you to tell the truth. Can't you see there is no one to speak for *him*, and I am his daughter. How could he do such a thing to Aunt Liss if he really loved her?"

"Then I had better tell you," said Emmy Lee quietly. "Come and sit down."

As I listened to her calm voice carefully telling me the whole pitiful story, explaining to me how it had happened, there was no doubt left in my mind that Mrs. Owen's words were true.

"But *why* couldn't he have waited longer for Aunt

Liss?" I cried. "She could have got better if she'd had her wedding to look forward to, couldn't she?"

Emmy Lee shook her head. "I don't know," she sighed. "I don't know. He was a gentle young man your father, weak perhaps and easily influenced. And your mother was very beautiful and gay and very strong-willed—she always managed somehow to get what she wanted. You mustn't blame him too much."

"My mother was to blame. Is that what you are telling me? She stole him from Aunt Liss!"

Emmy Lee got up and went back to slicing her onions, her face grim.

"That's not for me to say," she answered quietly. "It's over and done with long ago. Best try to forget it all."

Forget it all—how could I?

I fought down my shame and anger and tried to make excuses for my mother, but the icy finger of truth lay on my heart. I knew at last what she had done to Aunt Liss—her own sister. I felt my scalp tingling with shock, and in those few minutes I think I grew several years older. Such treachery was unspeakable, unbelievable, but I knew that Emmy Lee had told me the truth. This was the mother I had worshiped for so long. Could she really be such a despicable person? It was then that the radiance with which I had surrounded her began to fade, and my love for her to shrivel.

I sat on in the kitchen, sick at heart, and had my supper with Emmy Lee, for I felt that I could not yet face Aunt Liss without showing the burden of my new knowledge.

# CHAPTER FOUR

I WAS NOT ESPECIALLY HAPPY AT SCHOOL, AND NO ONE seemed to notice me particularly. I was careful to work enough to keep in the middle of the class and to avoid drawing the attention of the staff to me. Among the girls I was considered rather odd, mainly because I did not share in their whispered excitements; I had learned at home to keep my thoughts to myself. I got on well enough with them to avoid comment, but there was none of them I wanted to call my special friend.

But three times a week I came alive for an hour and stepped into another world, the absorbing vivid world of ballet. There I was happy, free, completely myself.

Oh, the joy of that one brief hour three times a week. My two worlds were kept discreetly apart; and it was abundantly clear from the attitude of my headmistress that she did not approve of the ballet, and it was never mentioned.

My mother never came near me nor the school, although she was often in London. A story grew up and spread that she was an eccentric painter who mixed only with other artists on her rare visits to London. It was not true, of course, but it saved my face and protected me from the curious. It also explained why she never appeared at school functions.

One summer holiday my Aunt Briony came over from Canada bringing her daughter, my cousin Miranda, who was a few years younger than I.

I had heard a lot about Aunt Briony from Aunt Liss and Emmy Lee. She had trained as a nurse and had met her Canadian husband in a hospital in 1916 during the war. I found her a gay, charming person, and it made Aunt Liss happy to have her in the house. Even my mother became a little more approachable during her visit, and as Emmy Lee remarked, there was laughter and lightheartedness in the house again.

For Miranda and me the summer passed happily in the endless small pursuits of children. We played on the nearest beach, searching for crabs under the long seaweed, teasing the sea anemones in the rock pools, fishing from the rocks in the deeper water when the tide was low, and waiting for the seals who came into the bay to play. Sometimes we helped Rees on the neighboring farm with the young calves, or played with Mrs. Owen's wild creatures. And always, when we were hungry, there was something to eat, warm from the oven, in Emmy Lee's hospitable kitchen.

Before they sailed for home, Aunt Briony suggested that I should visit them in Canada the following summer. When I sounded out Aunt Liss about it, she seemed embarrassed and I wondered why, till I discovered that although the Old Court belonged to her, she had very little actual money. My mother kept a tight hand on the Grenville funds, such as they were, and it was becoming increasingly difficult to get her to part with a penny of it, or of her own money, which her godmother had left her.

I went back to school almost as soon as they had gone, and when I came at Christmas time things had sunk into their old ways and the atmosphere was tense. My mother shut herself away in her studio for days on end, and Emmy Lee had to set her meals on trays, which I took up for her and left outside her door on the top floor.

I felt sorry for Aunt Liss, who missed our summer visitors, and I tried to be with her a great deal. I pushed her out sometimes in her wheel chair, when the weather was mild enough, accompanied by old Sergeant. We grew even closer together as I became older and more companionable to her, and there were many times when we were able to laugh and be happy together, our troubles forgotten.

But my mother resented those times. Although she would not join in with us, she was jealous and showed it in her barbed remarks to me.

One mild day in early January I had taken Aunt Liss round the garden. The sky was gentle and blue, the jasmine, like pale sunshine, spilled its gold down the old wall. I was wearing a new sweater of the same color.

"Go and try to persuade your mother to come out with us, it is so lovely," said my aunt, and I left her for a moment and ran to the house, my foolish heart hopeful as always.

I hurried to the top floor and knocked at the door. "Do come out in the sunshine with us, Mother," I urged as I stepped inside.

She was sitting in the window, in the sun, and wore a startled look, as if I had wakened her abruptly from a sleep, or a dream, and in her arms, hugged to her breast, was that loathsome wooden doll.

Something despairing in her pose impelled me closer to her, and I ran towards her holding out my hands.

"Do come out with us, it is so lovely," I entreated.

But even as I spoke, I knew it was no use. Her expression changed to one of contempt, and she turned on me. "Get out of my room," she said vindictively. "You look quite repulsive in that color!"

I turned and fled, biting my lip to keep back the tears. I returned to the sunny garden and Aunt Liss. But the magic had gone from the day.

"She won't come. It's no use, she won't even try to like me!" I gulped. "I don't believe she loves anyone in the world except that beastly doll!"

The words slipped out before I could stop them, but

the effect on Aunt Liss was startling.

"What did you say?" she asked sharply. "A doll? *What* doll?"

"A wooden doll, with a polished wicked face—a horrible doll!" I retorted.

"Dear Heaven! It must be Dido!" exclaimed Aunt Liss. She looked shaken and upset. "I have always wondered what became of her—your mother must have kept her hidden all these years. I hoped she had forgotten her."

"Forgotten her? I don't believe she'll ever do that," I said bitterly, and I told Aunt Liss how I had found Dido hidden in the hole in the ash tree.

"She doesn't hide her there any more," I said. "I think Mother keeps her in her studio. She paints pictures of her, you know. Dido is her model."

Aunt Liss started, and I saw her shiver. "How horrible," she said. "Poor Judith."

"Where did Dido come from?" I asked. "How did my mother get hold of such an extraordinary doll, extraordinary and horrible and—wicked!"

"She was in the house when we came here," said Aunt Liss, "in an old trunk in the attic. To your mother she was attractive, fascinating, from the start, so much so that she stole her from Aunt Briony, who found her in the first place. Judith always loved the unusual, the fantastic, the macabre."

"Aunt Briony liked Dido?" I cried in disbelief. "How could she?" The thought of my jolly, healthy, extremely normal aunt having any interest in that horrible doll was ridiculous.

"Oh yes," Aunt Liss insisted, "Aunt Briony came under Dido's spell all right in the short time she kept her. She was quite little then, but she was brokenhearted when the doll disappeared. Judith spirited Dido away."

"How can a doll be wicked?" I asked.

"It might have been made by someone evil, and so have the power of rousing evil in anyone who loves it," said Aunt Liss.

"But *how* does it?" I persisted. "Do you mean that Dido belonged to an evil person and absorbed wickedness from that person as an article of clothing absorbs the smell and personality of its wearer?"

"Maybe something like that," said Aunt Liss. "Perhaps there was even a bit of witchcraft in it."

"Witchcraft?" I breathed, and I felt the skin of my scalp prickle. "Do you think that someone in the family, old Aunt Lucia who left you the house perhaps, dabbled in witchcraft, even *was* a witch?"

Aunt Liss laughed. "Well, hardly Aunt Lucia," she said. "Probably someone long before her time, in the days when witchcraft was a very real and terrifying belief among country people. Dido may have belonged to some servant of this family, or someone awaiting trial for witchcraft. This was a courthouse long ago, you know. All kinds of evil people must have been tried within these walls. Dido could have belonged to one of them. It is the only explanation I can find for her. How I wish we could get the creature away from your mother," Aunt Liss concluded. "But I don't know what might happen if we tried."

"We'll never get the chance," I answered. "My mother is much too careful."

And we never did get the chance. I never saw Dido again. But from that day I began to suspect that my mother was slightly mad.

# CHAPTER FIVE

THE YEARS WENT BY, AND AS THE TIME DREW NEAR FOR me to leave school, the question of my future came up.

I could not get my mother to listen to my plea to be allowed to train as a ballet dancer. She simply would not hear of it, and I wondered how Aunt Liss had persuaded her to pay for my ballet lesson.

It was the one thing I knew I could do, the one thing I wanted to be, a dancer; but until I found a way to finance myself (for Aunt Liss could not help me) I decided I must live at home. I knew that when I was twenty-one I would have some money of my own from my father's estate. I might have to wait till then. Apart from that, I felt that Aunt Liss needed me. With my mother becoming progressively more unbalanced, I knew that it was too much for Emmy Lee to manage without my help. But I could still practice and keep my limbs supple, and this I did daily. Miss Julie had long since left the district, and there was no good teacher near to help me.

I was glad to have finished with school, and I soon settled down to helping run the house, and making myself generally useful.

The invitation to go to Canada was renewed, but although my mother took no pleasure in my company, she would not let me go. However there was enough to fill my life. With occasional parties at nearby houses, or concerts and plays on the radio, I was tolerably happy. Mrs. Owen, who was now quite senile, had to be visited and cared for when Rees was at work, and time for reading had to be squeezed into the day or night. It sounds like a dull life in a tiny world, but I made myself content with it, biding my time. A year passed quickly and it was 1938. War clouds were beginning to mass on the horizon. I felt sure that if war came I would have my chance to break away from home, and I determined that I must not miss it.

I talked with Aunt Liss, and with Emmy Lee, and explained to them how I felt, so that they would be prepared when the time came.

"Of course you must go," said Aunt Liss, "when your chance comes; but we are happy to have you here with us at the Old Court for as long as you can stay, Emmy and I—and your mother."

I looked at her quickly, but her face was serene; she really believed what she had said.

Spring came early that year; even in mid-February when I stood on the hill looking down to the copses of trees in the valley, a mirage of green shimmered on the bare branches, promise of summer to come.

One evening I went to Mrs. Owen's cottage, and busied myself getting supper ready for Rees.

"Seen that new young chap at the Jenkins' farm, Miss?" he asked me when he came in.

"No, what new young chap?" I asked.

"Proper young fellow he seems; Polish they say."

"Polish?" I repeated. "What is he doing at the farm?"

"Come for a year, student of some sort I shouldn't wonder," said Rees.

A few days later when I went to the farm to collect the eggs, a stocky dark young man sat at the table in the kitchen, eating a sandwich.

"This is Bron," said Mrs. Jenkins, the farmer's wife. "I can never get my tongue round his whole name, and this is Miss Dilys Grenville who lives at the big house in the trees over there."

The young man jumped to his feet and bowed, "Bronislav Kostarski at your service," he said in remarkably good English. "I am very pleased to meet you Miss Dilys Grenville." His vivid blue eyes looked into mine as I shook hands with him, and the sweetness of his smile illumined for a moment his serious face—too serious for so young a man.

I felt my color rising as he looked at me, and my heart beat deafeningly.

"I have heard of you from Rees," I said. "I hope you are happy here?"

"It is a kind country, your Pembrokeshire," he answered. "I am pleased to be here."

He carried my basket of eggs to the gate; then, "Excuse me that I leave you," he said. "I have not already finished my work." And he bent and kissed my hand.

I walked home in a daze of glory.

In so short a time, the space of half an hour, my destiny took shape, my whole world changed. I had fallen in love.

For a time I told no one my secret but hugged it to myself in delight, in rapture.

At first our meetings appeared casual, though I made a point of going to the farm, on one pretext or another, just about the time Bron finished work.

Then he began to ask me to meet him. We talked, leaning over field gates in the evenings, and as I got to know him better, we planned walks on the hills, or bathing on the sandy beaches.

He was a fiery turbulent young man, tinder-tempered, and at times we had violent quarrels, and I swore never to speak to him again.

But always next time we met we made it up, and in a way our quarrels helped to forge a stronger link between us.

Often Bron spoke of his home in Poland, of his mother and sister, and of his father who was a landowner and wanted Bron to farm his own estate. Then his eyes would blaze, and I learned that he loved his family and his land with a fierce, passionate love.

"Soon I shall leave this land," he said. "My father is a great admirer of the British and made me come to agricultural school here, but when my training is finished, I shall go home, home to Poland."

My heart sank when he spoke like this. I knew how quickly the time would pass, and I would be left without him. How could I bear it?

Sometimes it was my turn to tell him of my hopes for the future, my ambitions, how I wanted to dance, to become a great ballerina. "But alas, there is no money till I am twenty-one," I cried. "Now I can only practice hard, but then I shall be able really to dance, to travel with a ballet company."

"You should come to learn in my country," said Bron. "There are several good Polish companies, and wonderful teachers. But my father fears war is coming soon. Perhaps neither of us will do what we plan in the end, who knows.

"You have a pretty name, Dilys," he said changing the subject. "I have never heard it before."

"It was my grandmother's name, my father's mother," I explained. "He was killed in the war, in 1918 just before I was born. He wrote in his will that Dilys was to be my name; it was his wish."

"I like it," said Bron. "It suits you, but I shall call you 'Dili.' No one else has called you that have they?"

I laughed happily. It was true, many people had called

me "Dilly," but only Bron pronounced it "De-Lee"; it was his own special name for me.

It was a summer of ecstasy and of despair, ecstasy when I was with him, despair when I thought of being parted from him when he left for Poland.

Aunt Liss and Emmy Lee guessed my secret, and since my mother was away a good deal that summer, I was eventually able to bring Bron home to the Old Court in his free time.

But when the first frost sparkled in the grass and the evenings began to darken toward winter, I was filled with terrible sadness, for although Bron talked of his plans for the future, he never suggested that I might have any part in them, and this must mean that I did not matter to him, he did not care enough for me.

Then one frosty evening as we walked back from the farm together, a car passed us. It was the station taxi, and in it sat my mother, returning from a visit to London.

I knew that she must have seen us, and such a feeling of sickness came over me that I stumbled and would have fallen had not Bron caught me in his arms.

"Dili! Dili! What is the matter?" he asked, his voice troubled. "You are as white as snow, and trembling. Are you ill? Whatever has upset you?"

"Hold me tight, Bron," I pleaded. "I'll be better in a moment." And as his arms closed round me, I felt the color flood back into my face, and in spite of the shock I had had, my heart began to sing. He was anxious about me, concerned for me. He must care after all.

"My mother is back. She passed us in that car," I said,

struggling to control my shaking limbs. "She must have seen us. She will spoil everything for me if she can. *Everything!*"

"Listen, Dili," said Bron. "She can spoil *nothing* for us. You and I . . . even if we have to wait a while, it will not be for long. Oh Dili! . . . I had not meant to say it so soon, not till I had made plans with my father . . . Dili, I love you. Can you ever love me enough to marry me? I want to take you home—home to Poland. I cannot bear to leave you, ever."

Such a tumult of happiness swept through me that for a moment I could not speak. Then I whispered in a funny cracked voice, not a bit like my own.

"I will never *let* you leave me, Bron, darling Bron! Of course I'll marry you. I love you enough now. I always have."

Gaily we took hands and danced back home along the rough country road, and for us it was paved with gold.

We slipped into the Old Court through the kitchen, and ran straight to Aunt Liss's room, where I could hear Emmy Lee pulling the curtains.

There was no need to tell them our news; they saw it in our glowing faces as we stood in the doorway, hand in hand.

There was only time to rush into their welcoming arms, both of us, before Bron had to get back to the farm to attend to the animals.

My mother did not appear for supper, but afterwards, feeling as brave as a lion, I went to tell her of our engagement.

For a moment there was dead silence. Then her lip curled and she said icily, "Marry a farm laborer? *My* daughter! Most certainly not! I never heard of such nonsense!"

I *hated* her then, and I turned and fled from the room lest she pierce the radiance that wrapped me round. Down to the kitchen I ran to find refuge in helping Emmy Lee to wash up the supper dishes.

"How we're going to miss you, dearie, Miss Liss and me, but it's a wonderful thing for you. He's a fine young man, and you'll be happy with him even if it is so far away. Maybe you'll get your dancing, too. Anyway you'll not be going for a while yet," said Emmy Lee. "There's plenty of time."

But as I lay in bed that night, living over again the wonderful day, thinking ahead into the future, I wondered whether Emmy was right.

Supposing what Bron's father said were true. Supposing there was a war. Bron would want to get home to Poland. That meant I would go too, *nothing* must part us now . . .

Maybe after all Emmy is wrong, maybe there is not plenty of time . . .

PART III  *MELISSA*

# CHAPTER ONE

"THERE'S A LETTER FROM DILLY FOR YOU, MISS LISS."
Emmy Lee's joyful voice broke in on my reverie as
I sat in my wheel chair gazing out of the window of my
room.

"Oh, Emmy!" I cried, my heart fluttering with pleasure and thankfulness and apprehension. "Quickly,
quickly. Give it to me!"

My hands were shaking as I tore open the thin foreign
envelope. There was a single sheet inside, I read it aloud.

"Darling Aunt Liss,
    Terrible things are happening here. Soon we may

have to leave the farm. I will send news when and if I can, but I can give you no address. Bron and I are well. I hope this letter will get through to you.

My love to you and Emmy,

Dilly."

The date on the letter was October, 1939, and now it was May of the following spring. It had taken seven months to reach us.

"Oh, Emmy," I groaned. "It is hopelessly out of date, and there is no way of knowing what has happened to them by now."

It was well over a year since Bron had been sent for urgently by his father, and Dilys had gone with him to Poland.

At first her letters were happy. She loved her new home, Bron's family, her life in a strange country, her ballet lessons in the nearby town, and above all she loved her husband.

"I miss you and Emmy Lee," she wrote, "and if I had more time I would feel homesick; but things here happen so quickly."

The end of Poland happened quickly too, for in three short weeks, less than six months after Dilys left home, the country was overrun by German Nazi troops, and there were no more letters, no news.

All through that first autumn and winter of the war we were desperately anxious for her safety. Emmy and I comforted each other, hoping that somehow Bron would be able to send her back to England, to escape himself with the Polish forces; that some message would come through to us. But the weeks passed and there was nothing, nothing. And now this belated, slim letter, hopelessly outdated which told us very little.

Emmy put a comforting hand on my shoulder as I held out the letter for her to read herself.

I felt utterly deflated and weary as the flutter of hope in my heart died down again. There was nothing I could do. I must reconcile myself to the idea that Dilly, our beloved Dilly, was lost to us for a while in the vast turmoil of war.

"Remember her promise, Miss Liss," said Emmy Lee as she handed me back the letter. "There will be another letter, or a message, I am sure."

"Yes, Emmy, yes, I hope so indeed," I replied; but my words had an empty ring.

I propelled my wheel chair across to my desk, after Emmy had gone back to her kitchen, and from one of its pigeon holes I extracted the slim packet of Dilly's letters.

I spread open the first one before me and reread it for the hundredth time. I had found it on my pillow just after she had gone, after the last hasty farewells had been said and she had driven off with Bron on their headlong dash for his home in Poland.

"Darling Aunt Liss," I read,

"I know you understand why I have got to go. I hate to leave you and dear Emmy Lee so suddenly, but Bron must go home at once; his father's message said, *come most urgently*, and I must go with him. We'll be married from his home immediately. I shall miss you and Emmy terribly, but I promise you that someday, somehow, I will come back to you.

> Dilly."

"Emmy is right," I thought. "I will remember your promise and will go on hoping, my precious Dilly."

I folded the new letter and put in into my pocket. The others I put away again in my desk.

My thoughts went back over the years, to the day in 1919 when Judith and the baby Dilys had arrived home from India.

The 1914 war was over at last. Carew had been killed in a naval action a few months before the end, before his baby daughter was even born.

What had their married life been like? I knew little about their time in India for Judith's letters home had been few, and from Carew I had never heard, never after the day he and Judith ran away together to get married and I had given up all wish of recovery. They had sailed for India almost at once, out of our lives, and but for the war they might have remained there always. Penbryn had been sold at the time of Sir David's death. There was nothing to bring them back.

The old feeling of desolation swept over me as I remembered the bitter sorrow of those early months. Why, oh why, had Carew done this to me? What madness had drawn him into Judith's unloving arms? What evil power did she have over him to compel him to act against his gentle nature? It was a mystery I had never been able to solve.

But Dilys, my Dilly, was his daughter, and I loved her as my own child.

I remembered the first time I had held her in my arms, how I had searched her infant features for a likeness to Carew and how I had wished she were indeed mine. She was a frail sickly baby, nervous and ailing, unwanted and uncared for by Judith. But Emmy Lee and I loved her all the time she lived with us at the Old Court—all those twenty years.

When Judith came down at lunch time I gave her Dilly's letter. She read it quite calmly and returned it to me without a word. But her eyes were restless, and I knew that we would hear her during the night, pacing about in her room or creeping down the stairs out into the open, and away over the hills.

She had taken the first shock of Dilly's departure apparently unmoved, but gradually we saw a change in her. Surprisingly, she was fretting, missing the daughter she had never loved.

As time went on, her painting became fitful, and her visits to London less frequent.

Since the death of her godmother, Judith had become a wealthy woman; but she never spent any money, except what she contributed to our living expenses. She never bought any clothes; she saw no one but Emmy and myself. Yet as she became more odd and eccentric, in some strange way she became more human, and I hoped that in time a reasonable companionship might grow up between us, and the past might be forgotten.

But there were bad times when she shut herself away on the top floor and would see no one. Emmy would hear her steady tread, round and round her room as if she paced out an endless circle. She would croon in a queer high voice, and mutter to herself or to her only companion, the odious wooden doll, Dido.

It was better on these occasions to leave her alone, for if Emmy tried to enter the room, Judith would erupt into a violent rage.

"She'll set the house on fire one day likely as not," said Emmy Lee, "playing about with them candles."

"Candles? Whatever do you mean Emmy?" I asked.

"When she's better from one of her bad turns, there's always candle ends, a dozen or more, in the wastepaper basket when I go in to clean the room," said Emmy.

"How extraordinary. There's electric light in her room; what does she want with candles?" I said. Then a thought came to me. "Perhaps she's afraid of the dark, Emmy, and burns a candle in the room for comfort. Poor Judith."

"Maybe," Emmy replied. "Maybe, but I don't think so. I shouldn't wonder if they have something to do with that doll."

"Something to do with Dido?" I repeated, puzzled. What possible connection could there be between the candle ends and Dido? I thought very hard for a moment, searching my mind, and a buried memory stirred and shifted a little . . . it was something I had read once . . .

something about . . . witchcraft. But I could not quite remember it. I felt like someone playing hunt-the-thimble. I was warm and getting warmer but the thimble eluded me.

"I wish I could persuade Judith to see our doctor," I said once again, but this she utterly refused to do, and became violently disturbed when I suggested it.

When I consulted him about her, he advised me to keep her at the Old Court as long as possible, where her own surroundings helped to give her security. No treatment could be given without her cooperation, and this she refused to give.

"The time may come when she'll have to be taken into a mental hospital," he said. "But not yet, not so long as she does no harm and you can manage her at home."

Somehow Emmy Lee coped with both of us.

# CHAPTER TWO

IT WAS DURING THE SECOND YEAR OF THE WAR THAT I LOST
one of my most faithful friends. Mrs. Owen, who had
been ailing for some time, had a stroke and was moved
into hospital.

She lingered only a week, and just before the end she
recovered her power of speech and Emmy went to see
her for me.

Emmy Lee was very quiet when she returned with
her news.

"She's gone, poor old woman," she said. "Well, I suppose it's the best thing for her. I'll see to the cottage, of
course, till Rees comes home from the war."

"Did she send me any message?" I asked.

Emmy frowned and looked a little embarrassed.

"Well, yes," she said. "But I think her mind was wandering and I doubt if she knew what she was saying—anyway, it doesn't make sense."

"Never mind about that, tell me what she said," I insisted.

"She said she sees you walking by a stretch of water, and there is a child holding you by the hand. You see, I told you it was nonsense," said Emmy.

But I remembered other things that Mrs. Owen had "seen," and I wondered.

One day the front door bell rang just after lunch, and when Emmy went to answer it a strange young man in Air Force uniform stood on the step asking to see me. His stocky figure and strong face made me catch my breath as he came into my room. For a moment I had thought it was Bron. I was sure he was Polish, and my heart started to hammer with choking intensity as I made him welcome and sent Emmy Lee for coffee and cakes.

His face was lined, his hair graying, and I wondered what anguish and loss he had suffered before he reached the safety of England.

He came straight to the point.

"Madame, I have news for you from your niece Dili," he said; and he drew from his wallet a crumpled envelope which he handed to me.

"Excuse me," I said as I opened the letter with hands that trembled.

"This is our good friend Jan Bednarz," I read.
"He can tell you all our news if he ever reaches
England. Do not grieve for me dear Aunt Liss. I
am with Bron, so in spite of everything I am happy.
                                        Dilly."

"You are Jan Bednarz," I said. "It is good of you to
come."

"I was at school with Bronislav and have been a close
friend and neighbor of his for years," said the young
man.

"Now tell me about Dilly and Bron," I begged. "Tell
me all you can."

Emmy brought in the coffee and sat down to drink it
with us while Jan told us all he could.

"It is more than six months since I saw them," he said. "It has taken me all this time to reach your country; I could not come directly you understand."

He told us that Bron was working with the Polish underground resistance movement, which by sabotage and every means possible was seeking to undermine and destroy the Nazis in Poland.

"But that is terribly dangerous work," I cried, horrified.

"It is work for brave men and women," said Jan quietly. "There are plenty of them in Poland like Bron and Dili."

I sent Emmy to find Judith and bring her to meet our new friend, but she had gone out on one of her wild prowls over the hills.

Jan told us of the terrible food shortages, the deportations of the young men and women to labor camps in Germany, the appalling persecution of the Jews by the Nazis, but I felt that he was sparing us and that everything was infinitely worse than he made it out to be. My heart sickened as I thought of the ghastly dangers and difficulties that Dilly and Bron must face every day.

I tried to persuade Jan to spend longer with us, to come and stay with us at the Old Court for part of his leave. I felt he was our only link with Dilys. When he had to go, Emmy Lee gave him a parcel of her home-made pies and a cake to take back to camp with him. We were lucky to live in the remote country, where we were always able to get some extra butter or eggs or milk from the farms, over and above our rations.

It was Jan's only visit to us. I saw his name on a casualty list a few weeks later. He had been killed on a bombing raid over Germany.

One night there was a fearful gale and out into the teeth of it went Judith full of glee. Emmy Lee and I could not stop her, and since Rees was away at the war, we had no one to send after her.

She did not return till the early hours of the morning. Emmy and I, having sat up all night, heard her fumbling at the door.

She dragged herself into my room, a wild-eyed creature, her face turned gray with fatigue, her drenched clothes sticking to her. She babbled something about hurting her foot and lying out in the icy rain for hours.

Emmy peeled off her sodden clothing—we had kept a good fire burning—wrapped her in a blanket like a child, and went to run a hot bath for her. But while she was gone, Judith limped across the room and collapsed onto my bed, and Emmy had to be content with packing her round with hot water bottles and forcing some brandy between her chattering teeth. When she went to ring the doctor, I moved across to the bedside in my wheel chair. I was shocked at her noisy breathing and her bad color, and I took her hand in mine hoping to comfort and reassure her.

Her eyes were wild and frightened, and suddenly she said in a harsh voice, speaking carefully, "Melissa, you must look after my . . . Dido for me."

"Where is she?" I asked. At once a sly look came over

her face, and without a word she turned away from me.

She did not speak again; and when the doctor arrived, he looked grave and shook his head over her.

"It's pneumonia," he said. "She's very ill indeed; too ill to move into hospital. I'll try to send a nurse at once."

Judith had lapsed into unconsciousness before the nurse arrived, and she died the next day.

When Emmy came to sort out Judith's things and clear up her room, she made a thorough search for Dido, but she could not find her. We had so many other things to think about that the doll was forgotten for a while.

So Emmy Lee and I were left alone in the rambling old house, and somehow we managed, just the two of us. But soon I found that there was not enough money to keep it going without Judith, and it looked as if we would have to shut it up and go somewhere else, or sell it. Sell the Old Court. It was unthinkable.

Then two things happened. First, we were asked to accommodate evacuees from a Welsh industrial town, bombed out of their homes. A worn young mother with two lots of twins under four, moved in. That was the first thing. The second was so surprising that at first I could not believe it. I had a letter from a firm of London solicitors informing me that Judith had left me all the money she had inherited from her godmother. The Grenville money was held in trust for Dilys, of course, when we could find her, but this legacy had been Judith's personal wealth to do with as she liked, and she had left it to me. It was a considerable sum—almost a fortune. I felt that someone must have made a mistake, and I wrote to the solicitors, but their reply left no room for doubt. Judith had intended me to have the money from the day she herself inherited it. "She said she owed it to you," wrote the solicitor.

I thought over the words carefully. Had Judith possessed a conscience after all? Was she trying to compensate me for stealing Carew away all those years ago?

I shall never know, but I can't pretend that I wasn't glad to have the money and grateful to Judith for her surprising generosity. It meant I need never again have any financial worries. I insisted that Emmy Lee must share my good fortune—goodness knows she had earned it by her devotion to Judith all these years—and I handed her over as substantial a lump sum as I could make her accept.

Once Judith's affairs were all settled, there remained only one other thing to be done, to find and burn the horrible wooden doll, Dido.

But although Emmy Lee hunted, not only in Judith's room but all through the house from attic to cellar, as carefully as if she were looking for a coronet of diamonds, no trace of the doll could be found. We even sent one of the farm boys up the old weeping ash to search in the hole that had once been her hiding place, but he found nothing there except a handful of withered leaves.

Great clumps of the gray antlered Santolina, with its rank-smelling yellow flower had grown up round the bottom of the tree, and this we got the boy to cut and clear away. No Dido was hidden in its pungent thicket, nor anywhere in the garden.

"I believe Judith hid her somewhere on the hill, safe from us," said Emmy Lee.

But I did not agree with her. I felt certain that Dido must be in the house, somewhere where she could be discovered, or Judith would not have asked me to look after her. Emmy must search again.

But although another hunt was made, particularly in Judith's room at the top of the house, the room that had once been mine, no trace of the doll could be found and finally we gave up the search.

When they had been with us for a year, the elder pair of twins of our evacuee family was ready to begin lessons, and I started them off on their ABC's. Soon they were joined by the next two, and I discovered in myself a belated gift for storytelling, which held the four solemn little faces, round-eyed with interest.

Their mother, Gwenny, helped Emmy Lee in the house and garden, and worked part-time in the canteen at the harbor six miles away. Gwenny had changed from a scared worn waif, nerve-wrecked from air-raids and burdened with children, into a strapping rosy-cheeked country girl, and I often wondered if her husband, Evan Jones, would recognize her at all when he returned from the Japanese prison camp in Malaya.

Meanwhile, his family wove itself into our lives, and with children in the old house again, even our drab wartime pattern of life was shot with gold.

# CHAPTER THREE

AT LAST THE WAR DRAGGED TO AN END. GWENNY AND the children went back to the city to get a home ready for Evan Jones' return, and once again Emmy and I were left on our own. But soon Rees came back to his cottage, grayer-haired and more silent than ever. He took up his usual chores around the house, and the garden blossomed anew under his loving hand.

"Perhaps we shall hear from Dilys now; perhaps she'll come home here for a while. We must get the house ready for her," I thought, and I got in painters and chose new curtains, and Emmy Lee polished the old furniture till it shone. But Dilys did not come, nor was there any word from her.

At first I waited with expectancy, watching daily for
a letter, a message of some sort, but none came. Then I
began to try to trace her through the Red Cross, the
refugee organizations, the camps for displaced persons.
My enquiries were met with kindness and patience, but
it was like searching for one flake in a snowstorm. There
were thousands and thousands of lost and homeless
people in Europe, I was told, nameless numbers, unwanted, forgotten, discarded.

I had never until then acknowledged to myself that
Dilys might not even be alive. If she were, surely she
would find some way of sending a message to me?

As the weeks passed and nothing came from her, and
no trace could be found of her, my hopes began to sink,
but still I clung to the promise she had made: "Someday,
somehow, I will come back to you."

My anxiety over her and my deep sorrow as I accepted
the possibility that she was gone forever, began to affect
my health. I could neither eat nor sleep. The dreary
winter months set in, a winter of hard frosts and snow
blizzards, and my spirits fell to zero. But unknown to
me, and in desperation at my low state, Emmy Lee wrote
to Briony in Canada; and when after Christmas a letter
came from her proposing that they visit us in the spring,
she and Miranda, I took heart and began to recover.

There was a day in January when Rees pushed me out
into the garden. The jasmine hung down the wall in a
cascade of icicles, each golden spray encased in a sparkling sheath. I looked across the fields of shadowed snow.

glittering in the sunshine, to the gray expanse of sea beyond. It was the same old familiar landscape that I saw, but it was transformed by the whiteness of the snow into a startling new beauty.

I came home uplifted and hopeful once more, feeling that even in my life there could be a new chapter, a transformation.

They arrived in April, and it was wonderful to see them again.

"Liss! How you have shrunk!" cried Briony.

"Wartime feeding, in spite of those wonderful food parcels you sent us," I said, laughing.

"Wartime?" snorted Emmy Lee. "That's long past. You've been ill, tormented by grief over Dilly, why not say so? There's nothing of you. I can pick you up like a child."

Miranda had grown into a charming young woman, married and with two children left behind in their Canadian grandmother's care.

To her who had been Dilly's friend and contemporary, I found I could talk. It was an enormous relief and comfort to me. Together we were able to remember the little things, to laugh over memories of that happy summer in the Old Court, when they were children together.

"Oh, Miranda!" I cried. "Where *is* Dilly? Surely if she were alive, she'd have sent us some message, even if she could not come herself? If only I knew what had happened to her."

Miranda took both my hands in hers.

"You must stop tormenting yourself, Aunt Liss," she

said. "Dilly is gone, and I don't think we will ever know what happened to her."

I could not agree with her. There was a thread of certainty deep within me, that this was not the end of Dilly's story.

Before they went back, Briony and Miranda tried very hard to persuade me to go to Canada with them, Emmy Lee too, of course; but for me to leave the security of the Old Court was impossible. I could not do it, not then.

"You'd have a new life, new interests, meet new people," urged Briony.

"You'd love our children," said Miranda. "Do come."

I thanked them, but I could not go with them.

"This is my place," I said. "I must stay here in this house that I love. It has something for me—I must wait for it."

It was the end of the summer when they left, and Emmy Lee and I were alone in the house once more, except for Briony's parting present to me, a new young dog, called Gillie, who reminded me of my faithful old Sergeant. Although I missed them intolerably at first, their visit had given me new hope; it had restored my confidence in myself, and I knew I would not falter again.

I thought a great deal about Miranda after she had gone back. I felt deeply grateful to her because she had brought Dilly close to me again. I held the photos of Miranda's two children in my hands and searched their faces for family likenesses. If only Dilly had had a child. This was something I had never thought of before. Why had it never occurred to me? Perhaps Dilly and Bron did have a child.

It was such a tremendously exciting, significant possibility that I felt new life pulsing through my veins and a whole new world spreading out before my eyes.

For the next few days this thought was constantly in my mind, waking and sleeping. I pondered and dreamed of nothing else. Did Dilly have a child?

Then one evening I had an astonishing experience.

Emmy Lee had lighted the fire in the drawing room, which we had been using during Briony's visit. I had finished my tea and was sitting alone in the dusky room, a book on my knee and Gillie stretched on the rug beside me. Dreamily, I let my eyes rest on a golden shaft of the evening sunlight which lingered on the wall of the room, and just for a second, caught as if netted in the beam, I saw the face of a child.

It was gone in an instant, and I smiled at the trick my imagination or the light had played on me; yet the illusion pleased me so much that I felt quite elated.

A few days later, the same thing happened again, but this time the morning sunshine flooded my room as I sat at my desk, and for an instant there, hung in a sunbeam, was a child's face, nebulous, the features hazy . . . then it was gone.

After that it appeared at irregular intervals, sometimes not for several days, sometimes for two or three days running, and always when I was alone. I would suddenly look up, and there for a moment would be the face. It never stayed for more than a second, but I found

myself expecting to see it and feeling disappointed if it was not there.

I did not mention it to Emmy Lee, for I knew she would tease me and try to explain it away, and I did not want this.

Then gradually the features became more distinct each time the face appeared, until I was able to recognize in it a likeness to Carew. Yet it was not quite Carew as I had known him, but rather as he might have been as a child of five or six.

This phantom child was a great comfort and joy to me, and as the weeks went by I grew to love the face. I pretended to myself that there was a real child in the house again.

After a time, when I had grown entirely familiar with the little ghost or whatever it was, I realized that the face had changed since I first saw it; gone was the roundness of the early months, the features were becoming more pronounced, in fact the face of the child was growing older.

I began to take the whole thing more seriously, to try to find some explanation. Was it entirely in my own imagination, a phantom child of my own mind?

Was there a ghost in the house, a gentle friendly child with Carew's face?

Or was there a real child somewhere whose yearning to be in the Old Court was so strong, so intense, that he was able to project an image of himself, a sort of telepathic picture on the air of the house? The idea was fantastic and I dismissed it.

Nevertheless my preoccupation with the child kept me going while the search for Dilys still went on. So far every effort had failed, and I was becoming reconciled to her loss.

I had not told Emmy Lee anything about the child, but finally I could keep him to myself no longer. He had become almost an obsession; he was the only important thing in my life. I had to share him, talk about him, to keep my sanity.

I chose an evening when we sat in the sunny garden after tea—his appearances were always in the house and, so far as I knew, only to me—and I told Emmy Lee the whole story.

Her face changed from incredulity at first, through concern to bewilderment, and I could see that she was at a loss as to what to make of it; for she stabbed the needle into her darning with ferocity.

"You've never seen him have you, Emmy?" I asked her.

She shook her head violently.

"Me? Oh no. No. Never!" she said, and I saw her shiver slightly.

"I'm perfectly sane and in complete control of myself, Emmy," I said calmly. "So don't start telling me that I am out of my mind."

She chuckled as if I had taken the words out of her mouth before she spoke them.

"Well, whatever it is, ghost or fairy tale, I don't care; but this I *do* know, it is doing you good. You're a different person; there's some life about you now, so I have no quarrel with it, whatever it is." She gave me a penetrating look that ended in a smile, and I was glad that I had told her.

"It must seem absurd that the appearance of a child's face in the house has given me a new interest in life," I said, "but it is so. And there is something more, Emmy. I feel as if I were waiting for something to happen, something tremendous, something that will make all the pieces of this strange puzzle fall into place."

# CHAPTER FOUR

A WEEK OR TWO LATER THE NEW VICAR'S WIFE CAME TO tea and we sat talking by the fire till nearly six o'clock. She left a warm friendliness in the room when she went, and I was sitting thinking over our conversation, when my young dog Gillie began to whine and howl in his sleep. At the same moment the child's face appeared in the room and for the first time the eyes were looking straight at me. I stared back at him, willing him to stay, holding him, compelling him, but I was terrified that the dog would scare him away. I dared not move my eyes even for a moment, so to quiet Gillie I nudged him with my foot.

*I nudged him with my foot!*

For a moment I thought I was going to faint with shock, then tentatively, I managed to move my foot again. It was a tremendous effort, but I succeeded. I did it. After all those years of helplessness I could move my foot!

It couldn't be true. It was impossible, unbelievable. But it was true. I blew my nose to make certain that I was not dreaming, and I took two or three deep breaths to calm my thudding heart. Then joy came flooding over me as I saw new and wonderful vistas opening ahead of me; and wildly, frantically, I began to call—"Emmy Lee. Emmy Lee. Come. Come quickly!"

She came running at the urgency in my voice, her face anxious, and stood gaping at me speechless as I babbled—"Look. Look! I can move my foot. Emmy, *I can move my foot!*"

"After all those years!" she gulped at last. "It's a miracle," and she took both my hands in hers and burst into tears.

"It might not mean very much," I reminded her, trying to calm myself. "We can't tell till the doctor has seen me; then we can make plans. I'll ring him tomorrow morning. But for tonight let's savor it together, just you and me, Emmy."

After she had bustled off to get our supper, I sat on in the firelight, excited and happy, and suddenly the child's face was there before me again, more clearly than I had ever seen him. And again the eyes looked straight at me and I suffered a second shock, for al-

though there was a distinct likeness to Carew, which I
had long since recognized, the eyes that now regarded
me solemnly and intently did not remind me of him—but
of Dilly.

Then the head turned for a moment, and I saw that
the hair at the back was held in position by a ribbon. I
had been mistaken all along; the child's head was not a
boy's but a girl's.

I went to bed early that night, for I was tired out with
all the excitement; but I was not able to sleep. My
thoughts were in a turmoil, my mind racing with wild
plans of all the things I would do if I was going to be
able to walk again, and somewhere at the core of my
hopes was this unknown child. Where did she come
from? What did she mean?

I heard the slow ticking of the clock as the hours of
the night staggered by, and still my thoughts hovered
round the child. Why had she come? The answer was
just out of my grasp, just beyond my understanding.

I must have dropped off to sleep, for suddenly I woke
with a start and thought Dilly was in the room with me,
so compelling and vivid was the image of her in my
dream. I thought I heard her voice repeating the words
of the promise she had made me in the letter: "Someday,
somehow, I will come back to you."

It was not yet quite light, and as I lay waiting, I heard
the cool clear notes of an early curlew. They fell like a
benediction on my troubled mind.

And suddenly, at that moment, I understood, and with
such certainty that without realizing the voice was mine,

I spoke the words aloud.

"She is Dilly's child, Dilly's daughter . . . She must be . . . She's lost . . . and I have got to find her."

Relief surged up in me. However fantastic the idea might appear, I knew that I was right. This child was Dilly's daughter, lost in some camp for displaced persons, some home for refugee children. The pieces of the puzzle slid into place, and by the time Emmy Lee came in with my breakfast, I had made my plans.

Emmy could only shake her head incredulously at my extraordinary notion.

"Well, I don't know," she said, "it's the queerest thing I've ever heard; but if it gets you properly on your feet again, I'll believe anything you say."

"Emmy, I will find that child, if it's the last thing I do, if it means visiting every orphanage or camp for lost children in Europe."

Emmy looked gravely at me. "Yes, Miss Liss," she said. "I believe you will."

"Now please go and ring the doctor and ask him to come and see me as early as he possibly can," I said. "I shall write to my solicitor today and get him to begin the search for the child."

It took me a year, a year of struggle and disappointment, a year of determination and perseverance, to learn to use my legs again so that I could walk.

The medical people were wonderful in their patience with me, and but for their sympathy and encouragement, I think I would have failed.

There were months of visits to the hospital for treatment, massage and physiotherapy, till gradually the wasted muscles began to work and my legs became strong enough to bear my weight.

Then came the effort of learning to keep my balance and then, at last, I managed to take a few unsteady steps.

This was a wonderful achievement, and I found it difficult to believe that I was not dreaming. To be able to walk again after years in a wheel chair. It was staggering. I was full of hope and determined to go on trying until I could walk like anyone else.

Soon I could cross the floor with the help of two canes and each day I walked a little further.

Emmy Lee helped me in every way she could and watched my improvement with joyful incredulity.

But I was saving the final surprise for her. Alone in my room, with the door shut, I learned to discard first one cane and then the other and to walk a few steps at a time unsupported.

And at last the day came when I felt confident enough to walk without help across the room several times, and I knew that now I must tell Emmy Lee and show her that I was ready for what I had to do.

I chose a morning when she had gone shopping, and I listened for the bus bringing her back from the village. I heard it stop at the end of our drive and start again. Then from my window I saw Emmy and her shopping basket come through the garden gate. I knocked and beckoned to her as she crossed towards the front door. She nodded and smiled and in a moment she had dumped her heavy shopping basket in the entrance hall and was tapping at my door.

"Come in, Emmy," I cried.

She stood stock still in the doorway, a tremulous smile on her face and her eyes shining. I walked steadily across the room towards her.

"Miss Liss," she whispered, in a voice that was not quite steady. "Miss Liss. You've done it! You're a miracle. A bloomin' miracle!"

"Dear Emmy," I said, "I'm ready now. We will go abroad, you and I, to look for that child until we find her."

PART IV  *NINA*

## CHAPTER ONE

SHE WAS A TALL THIN LADY WITH GRAY HAIR AND SHE walked with a cane, an elegant black cane with a silver handle.

She stood with our house mother in the middle of the room, and her eyes searched carefully, intently, round the faces of the children, till they stopped at me.

"This is the child," she whispered to our house mother, and she came towards me slowly, expectantly, like a traveler who has come to the end of a journey.

Our house mother beckoned to me, "Come, Nina," she said, "I want you in my room for a little while. This lady, Miss Mansell, has traveled a long way to see you, all the way from England."

"Miss Mansell? From England?" I repeated, puzzled. "From England?" I stared at the lady with more interest, and the stories my mother used to tell me of her home in England rustled like leaves in my memory.

My house mother and the lady were engrossed in conversation as I followed them out of the room and into our house mother's study. I felt shaken, suspicious and a little frightened. What did this mean, and who was the lady? What had she come for? What did she want of me?

"Miss Mansell wants to talk to you," our house mother explained. "She used to know your mother when she was a girl in England."

"My mother did live in England once," I said guardedly. "In a place called . . . Wales." I spoke English a little haltingly. I was somewhat out of practice, although my mother and I had always talked in her native tongue.

"What was your mother's name?" asked the old lady.

"Madame Rolska," I answered, "but my father called her Dili." A light came over Miss Mansell's face, and she continued eagerly, "Do you remember the name of the village or of the house where your mother lived in England?" she asked. I shook my head. I could not remember. But I liked the lady and wanted to help her, so I went on.

"It is more than two years since my mother died, and before that for a long time, about five years I think, she was ill and she could not remember names. But she used to talk to me a great deal about her home in England—

the tall old house, the garden with the great tree, the
birds on the high moors, and the sea. I feel I know it all
quite well, she spoke of it so often, but the names I do
not know."

"What else did she tell you?" asked the lady.

"Oh, about the people, the people she loved, Aunt Liss
and Emmy Lee. My name is Melissa, you know, Nina
Melissa. I am called after Aunt Liss."

The tall lady rose to her feet, and I saw that she was
trembling.

"I am Melissa Mansell," she said. "I am Aunt Liss."

"You are Aunt Liss?" I repeated dazedly. "Did you say *you* are Aunt Liss?"

I stared at her unbelievingly and shook my head.

"Oh, no, you c-can't be *our* Aunt Liss," I stammered. "There is some mistake. Our Aunt Liss was an invalid. She was not able to walk, mother said so. I saw a snapshot of her once in an invalid chair. I remember it."

The lady nodded. "It's perfectly true," she said. "All the years your mother lived with me, I was an invalid in a wheel chair, but now as you can see I have recovered the use of my legs. I had to, so I could come to look for you, Nina. And now I have found you."

"We have been trying to find your Aunt Liss for a long time," said our house mother. "And she has been trying to find you, Nina. Only within the last few weeks have we made any contact, and not till today have we been quite certain."

"How did you manage to find me now?" I asked curiously.

"We have been trying to trace the relatives of Nina Rolska," our house mother explained. "But Rolska was not your father's real name."

"His name was Bronislav Kostarski," Aunt Liss broke in. "Your mother, who was my niece Dilys, married Bronislav Kostarski, and this is the name *I* have been trying to trace."

I looked from one face to the other in bewilderment. I had never known this. What did it mean? My house mother smiled reassuringly and patted my shoulder.

"It is all right, Nina," she said. "We now know that

your father changed his name during the war. Many
people had to do this to escape death. His own name
was too well known to the Gestapo, the German secret
police, who were hunting for him. He was a brave man,
your father; he worked in the Polish Resistance. Had the
Germans known who he really was when they caught
him, he would have been shot at once. We know that he
and your mother were taken to a concentration camp in
Germany. By changing his name he saved both their
lives, and after the war they found one another again and
then you were born."

"But how did Aunt Liss find me with all this confusion
over names?" I asked.

"When all our attempts to trace your relatives had
failed, we finally put an advertisement in the personal
column of an English newspaper," said our house mother.
" 'Will Aunt Liss who lives in Wales communicate with
us at once.' It was a remote chance, but it worked. Do
your remember when I asked you about your Aunt Liss?"

"I had searched for you so long and in so many places
I was almost in despair," said Aunt Liss. "Then, by
chance, I saw the advertisement in an old copy of the
newspaper. You can imagine the rest."

I could not quite believe that this was really happen-
ing to me. I felt dazed, as one does after a strange dream.
It had all happened too quickly and unexpectedly. I
needed time for belief.

Our house mother came to my rescue. She understood
that I was out of my depth; and she must have noticed
the telltale pallor of Aunt Liss's face.

"Your aunt is staying quite near here, Nina," she said, "and will be coming to see you again tomorrow. I think you should say good night to her now and join the other children."

"Oh yes," I said, glad to escape from this bewildering situation into my familiar surroundings. "It will be lovely to see you again tomorrow . . . Aunt Liss."

"I hope you will come back to England with me, Nina, in a month or so, home to the Old Court, my house and your mother's home. Will you think about it?" said Aunt Liss.

I nodded and slipped out of the room.

I did not join the other children, not even Anya who was Polish and my special friend. I had to be alone for a little while. I went up to the bedroom I shared with three other girls, climbed up onto the window sill beside my bed, and curled up behind the curtain out of sight.

I shut my eyes and thought of the old house, my mother's home, where I had so often been in my imagination. I wandered from room to room, remembering every detail, which my mother's descriptions had printed indelibly on my mind. This house, the Old Court Aunt Liss had called it, had been my refuge for years.

My mother and I used to pretend we were living there in elegance and beauty. We played at filling the charming rooms with flowers and cleaning them with loving care, polishing the old furniture till it shone; we ate delicious food at the table in Emmy's kitchen; we sat by the fire in the drawing room, listening to music on the gramophone.

We wandered in the sunny sweet-scented garden, or over the moors, or down by the sea. It was a fascinating, wonderful game.

And it taught me how my mother had lived as a child, how one day I too might live.

I had asked her once why we did not go there. But she had only looked a little lost and said that it was too late for her. Even then, I had understood at least in part what she meant.

Yet the old house remained our escape from the squalid camps for lost people, for the homeless, where we lived. It was a lighted candle in a dark room. And after my mother's death, when I was sent to the orphanage, alone in the world, I could still imagine myself living in my mother's old home with Aunt Liss.

Often I had wished that she could have told me the names and the places before her mind had become confused and muddled. I knew, now that I had seen Aunt Liss, that it would have been impossible for my mother to go back to her, back to the Old Court, the place she had loved. She wanted Aunt Liss to remember her as she was when she left home, before the war years had left their mark.

We moved from one camp to another, for she was very restless and could not settle. Then she fell ill, very ill. It was the end; she did not recover.

After her death there was no record of who she was and where she came from, only our names, "Dilys and Nina Rolska—Polish." I was ten then, one of the hundreds of lost children.

So, because I had never known last names, "Miss Mansell" meant nothing to me. But Aunt Liss—why Aunt Liss meant everything in the world. Of course I would go home to England with her and live in the old house and see for myself the garden and the moors and the sea, and all the things my mother had loved.

I felt more confident now, and I went down to find Anya and the other children at supper, to tell them my wonderful news.

# CHAPTER TWO

WE DID NOT GO STRAIGHT HOME TO ENGLAND. AUNT LISS
said we needed time to get to know one another, and
she took me to a lakeside village in Switzerland where
we stayed for a month, Aunt Liss, Emmy Lee and I.

Sometimes we drove through the low sheltered val-
leys scattered with spring flowers; or took the steamer
across the blue lake with its frame of shining snow peaks.

Once we made a shopping expedition to the little
town at the end of the lake, and Aunt Liss bought
clothes for me and shoes, and heaped presents upon me
until I wished she would stop. It was too much. The
contrast from my old life was too great.

Often I would stroll with Aunt Liss by the shores of the lake while we talked, or I would sit quietly with Emmy Lee while she sewed or knitted. Her hands were always busy, and I found great comfort in her presence; she was so undemanding, so reliable. Emmy was one of the kindest people I had even known. I could count on her to answer my sometimes difficult questions with truth and understanding; and it was she who taught me the little things that a girl learns from her mother, the small personal details of care and fastidiousness a young woman must know, a young woman beginning to live a normal life in a normal home.

As the end of the month approached, Emmy Lee went home to get the Old Court ready—it had been shut up for some time—and Aunt Liss and I were left alone. It was during this time, when we were beginning to know one another, that I was able to ask her a question that had been bothering me. How did she know about me?

She told me of her long long hunt through the Red Cross and other societies after the war ended, and of her despair and utter failure in finding any trace of my parents. The explanation, of course, was in the change of name, which I had not known about. Then it was my turn, and I told her the story of my life from the time my father died till I came to the orphanage, as much of it as I could remember, only leaving out the worst parts. "I can scarcely remember my father," I said. "But I know he was very ill, too ill to be moved, too ill to go to England or Poland or anywhere, and my mother would not leave him. After he died, we moved from one camp to another and my mother was ill in her mind. She was muddled and confused and forgetful."

"But why did she not write and tell me, so that I could have helped? So I could have brought you both home?" asked Aunt Liss.

This was a question I was not ready to answer, although I thought I knew why, so I only said, "She meant me to come home to you someday; she used to tell me so. 'It is too late for me, I have changed too much, I cannot go, but you must go home to Aunt Liss, Nina,' she would say. She was like a clock that has run down. She could not get going again, and she could not help me to find you. I think now that part of her died with my father."

Aunt Liss's face was drawn with grief. I wanted to spare her more pain, but she insisted that I finish.

"Go on, Nina," she said quietly. "Tell me the rest."

"There is not much more to tell," I replied brusquely. "My mother became like a child and had to be looked after constantly when her mind was completely gone. Her old illness—asthma she called it—came more often and grew worse. That is what killed her in the end."

"But who looked after her? You were only a child!" cried Aunt Liss.

"Our friends in the camp, many of them Polish, homeless refugees like ourselves, they helped me," I told her. "Only at the end she had to go to the hospital. After she died, those friends took care of me till I went to the orphanage."

I could see how painful all this was to Aunt Liss. The

picture was new to her and clear-cut. To me the edges
were blurred, the worst parts had faded and softened.
Even the sorrow of my mother's death had become bear-
able with the passing of time.

"But how did you know about me? How did you
know there was a me to come and look for?" I asked.

Then Aunt Liss said an amazing thing.

"You began to haunt my house," she said. "I saw your
face over and over again."

"Do you mean I was a sort of . . . ghost?" I asked,
feeling rather intrigued with the idea.

"You may call it that if you like," said Aunt Liss. "At
first I did not know who you were, or why I kept seeing you. Then I grew conscious of the fact that Dilly
might have had a child, and the thought grew in me
until I became certain that the face in the house was the
face of Dilly's daughter, your face, Nina. Your mother
made me a promise you know, when she married your
father and went to Poland with him just before the war:
'Somehow, someday, I'll come back to you,' she wrote.
She herself could not come, but I like to think that you
kept that promise for her; you came in her place, Nina."

I thought about this for a moment, and then I said,
"Perhaps it was because of the game I played, pretending
I lived in the house, imagining myself there with you,
so that I made a sort of impression, an image of myself
in the house . . . how very strange."

"Once I understood who you were, I knew I had to
go and find you," Aunt Liss continued.

"So you had to get up and walk again like one of the

miracles in the Bible!" I exclaimed.

"Yes," said Aunt Liss, "there had been nothing to live for, nothing to get better for all those years, but you changed that, Nina. When I knew that I must search until I found you, it gave a new meaning to my life. It has taken me a long time, but now I've done it."

I was very quiet for a while after she had finished speaking, thinking over the strange puzzling story. I smoothed it out in my mind and fitted the pieces together till the pattern was complete.

It was the end of a chapter, and I was ready to go on to the next.

I got up and walked over to Aunt Liss and slipped my hand into hers.

"Let's go home to the Old Court," I said. "Let's go home *now*."

# CHAPTER THREE

AUNT LISS HAD ORDERED A TAXI TO MEET US AT THE station the day we came at last to the Old Court. The driver shook hands with her as he helped her in.

"I intend to learn to drive myself," said Aunt Liss, "so that we can have a car of our own very soon."

"I don't mind being done out of a job by you, Miss," said the driver, laughing, as we drove off.

It was a gentle, kindly landscape of tiny, neat, patchwork fields. Set in the sheltered folds and dips, were the farms: sturdy stone buildings, each one with its surrounding bodyguard of trees. Whitewashed cottages, gay with painted woodwork, dotted the roadsides.

156

In about twenty minutes we turned off the main road, up a rough lane between the fields.

"There it is," cried Aunt Liss. "There is the Old Court."

I stared at the tall, whitewashed, stone house peering at me through its sentinel trees, its windows fringed with black paint. So this was the Old Court.

I had expected to recognize it, and I felt disappointed, for the house from the outside was completely strange to me.

My fancy was caught by the funny little round window high up under the roof, as if the old house was keeping an eye on the sea.

We drove past the garden wall, which shut off the front of the house, and drew up in the cobbled yard at the back.

Emmy Lee was waiting for us at the door and hurried to help Aunt Liss out of the car.

"Welcome home, dearie!" she cried holding out her arms to me.

Gillie, Aunt Liss's splendid dog, went nearly mad with delight at seeing her again; but I noticed how gentle he was with her, not jumping up against her as most dogs would, but showing his joy by leaping in the air and bounding round her in circles, and all the while keeping up a series of excited whinings, like a human conversation.

At last, he turned his attention to me and came and sniffed around me, deigning to wag his tail a little, but showing no enthusiasm. He was a gorgeous dog, but he never had much use for me when Aunt Liss was about. She was his queen.

As soon as we entered the house, I had a strange sense of recognition, a feeling of having been there before. I found that I knew where the different rooms on the ground floor were, and none of them was entirely strange to me; but Aunt Liss's sitting room I knew intimately, and it seemed to welcome me.

"Emmy has prepared your mother's bedroom for you, Nina," said Aunt Liss. "We thought you'd like to be there to begin with. If you'd rather have another room for your own, you can change, of course, after tonight."

"Thank you," I said. Emmy Lee picked up one of my suitcases and, beckoning with her head, she led the way upstairs.

"There now," puffed Emmy, throwing the door wide and dumping my case on the floor. "You'll want to wash. The bathroom is at the end of the passage, and my room is next door to yours. Don't be long. I'll tinkle the bell when supper is ready."

She bustled off, and I sat down on the bed and let my gaze wander round the room. It was fresh and pretty and miraculously white. I tried to imagine my mother at my age, sitting on the bed, or reaching up to hang her clothes in the cupboard, or standing by the bookshelf choosing a book; perhaps leaning out of the window, which opened onto the sunny garden, and trying to touch the great gnarled old tree that grew close to the house. The image of her rose sharply, stabbingly, in my mind, and the old familiar ache began to throb so pain-

fully that tears ran down my cheeks. This room could
never be mine. It reminded me too poignantly of her.
Here I would always be conscious of her, and my sense
of loss would be insupportable. If I was to start a new
life, it must be in a place of my own.

So while Emmy put the finishing touches to our supper, I hurriedly tidied my hair and washed my face and
hands, obliterating the traces of my tears, which I must
hide from Aunt Liss. In a moment I heard the tinkle of
the supper bell and ran gratefully downstairs.

Supper was laid at a window table in the kitchen, just
as in my mother's stories, and I noticed how the table,

silver, and glass gleamed with Emmy's care. The delicious smell that rose into the room when Emmy cut into her wonderful pie, made my mouth water. There were also bottled strawberries from the garden, and cream. When I had eaten as much as I could manage, I helped Emmy wash up while Aunt Liss went into her sitting room to drink her coffee. I carried it in to her and found that she had turned on the radio. I knew well this quiet room. My mother had imprinted every detail of it on my memory. It was here that we most often played our game, she and I, for this was the room she loved most, the room where Aunt Liss had lived her invalid life. I wandered round it, recognizing and remembering, touching the desk, the bookcases, the flower table, with caressing fingers. Then seeing that Aunt Liss was listening to a concert on the radio, I slipped out to ask Emmy Lee's permission to explore the part of the house I did not know.

"Of course, dearie," she said, and looked at me rather strangely. I thought she was about to say something more but she thought better of it.

I went straight to the top of the house and paused for a moment in the passage to get my sense of direction. Then I made for the farthest door. I found myself in an attic room, the very room I had hoped to find, for set high in the north wall was the round window I had already noticed from outside, the eye of the house that looked out to sea.

This room was entirely strange to me. I did not remember my mother having talked about it, and I could recognize nothing in it. It was painted white, and there were pretty, faded curtains and chair covers, and enough furniture for comfort, but it gave an impression of bareness, of austerity, which I liked. It seemed to have been unoccupied for a long time, and it smelled faintly, unpleasantly musty.

There was nothing cozy or warm about its atmosphere, rather the reverse. It had a queer repelling air of isolation, of independence, which somehow appealed to me; it excited me because it was different, and I decided then and there that this should be my room. I accepted its challenge, whatever it was.

I went downstairs to say good night to Aunt Liss and found Emmy Lee seated beside her, quietly knitting, and Gillie hunched on the floor between them.

"Well?" said Aunt Liss. "Are you ready for bed? You must be tired. Good night, my darling, and sleep well."

Shyly I bent to kiss her, and Emmy Lee rose to accompany me upstairs.

"Aunt Liss . . ." I began, "I'd like . . . you said . . . I mean, will it be all right if I change my room tomorrow and have the one at the top of the house, the one with the round window looking out to sea?"

Aunt Liss and Emmy glanced quickly at one another, and the expression on Emmy's face was one of consternation.

"Don't you like your mother's room?" asked Aunt Liss gently. "Would you really rather be all alone at the top of the house?"

I nodded confidently. "Yes. I can look at the sea from that room," I said. "I would like to have it for my own." I could not explain to her what I felt about my mother's room, nor why I was drawn to the other.

"Very well," said Aunt Liss. "It was my room once, before my accident. Then it was Judith's, your grandmother's room, where she used to paint her pictures. She used to shut herself away up there and sometimes we didn't see her for hours on end, days even."

"My grandmother?" I broke in. "So she was Judith? My mother's mother? What happened to her?"

"She died during the war," said Aunt Liss, shortly. "Did your mother talk about her to you?"

I shook my head. "Not very much," I said, trying hard to remember. "There was someone called Judith she feared and hated, but she did not talk about her. I did not know that Judith was my mother's mother.

"It was you she always spoke of, Aunt Liss, you were the one she loved."

I said good night and went upstairs with Emmy Lee to my mother's old room.

"Such a pretty room," said Emmy, chattily, as she folded the cover off my bed, "and close to me next door. I've never liked that other room, there's something about it . . ." She hunched her shoulders expressively. "Won't you change your mind and stay here, dearie?" she coaxed.

I shook my head and tried to explain to her a little.

"This was my mother's room," I said. "If I stay here, I shall miss her too much; but also, I am not my mother,

I am me, and I must have a place of my own."

"Very well," said Emmy, simply. "I'll get it ready for you tomorrow."

When she had gone and I had undressed and was ready for bed, I crept upstairs to the room on the top floor.

Moonlight streamed in through the window, enhancing its chill eeriness.

I strode across to the middle of the floor and announced in a truculent voice:

"I am Nina Melissa Rolska . . . no, Kostarska."— Which? I wavered and felt lost for a moment, then I continued: "I have come home to live in this house and this is my room—mine."

I could feel my heart thumping loudly in the utter silence that followed my announcement. I half expected to hear a shiver of mocking laughter, for I knew very well that this room was not empty—somebody, something, was already in occupation.

A piece of furniture gave a loud crack as if rousing itself from sleep, and I jumped as if I had been hit. A chill ran down my spine. I felt hostility like a bad smell seeping through the room, enmeshing me as if in a web. I knew I was unwelcome here, and yet there was an air of expectancy, as if the room had been waiting for someone, for someone resented but vital to it . . . waiting for *me?*

# CHAPTER FOUR

My first few days at the Old Court were spent in discovering and exploring the house and garden. I went by bus into the village of Newcove with Emmy Lee. I met the bent old gardener they called "Young Rees"; I wandered across the fields and down to the beach in the bay; and Emmy took me to collect the eggs from the farm where my father had worked before the war. I was fascinated by the old pebbled floor of what used to be the farm kitchen—round pebbles from the beach worn smooth with use, and firmly embedded in hard sand. "This is one of the old style floors," Emmy told me. "They are not made like this any more."

I helped Aunt Liss gather flowers from the borders in
the shelter of the old wall and arrange them in the different rooms of the house. I walked with her through the
orchard gate and up onto the moor, but it was all a little
unreal, as if I were living in a dream, and I missed Anya.
I was lonely for someone of my own age and with my
own tough background.

When my room on the top floor was ready for me,
scrubbed by Emmy and shining with polish, I moved
my belongings up there, stowed my clothes away in
drawers and cupboards, and took possession of it. The
windows were wide open, and I sat down on the deep
alcove seat under the round window, sniffing the air
from the sea and the smell of the polish, and something
else, that faintly musty smell, animal and earthy, which
I had noticed before. It was unpleasant and somehow
disturbing, and I wondered why it still lingered after
Emmy's scrupulous cleaning.

On my knee I held a small battered leather bag, kept
tightly closed by tasseled thongs slotted round the top.
In it I kept my relics, bits and pieces of treasures ac-
quired along my path: a brooch of my mother's and her
wedding ring bedded in cotton wool in a tiny cardboard
box; an ornamental comb; a string of colored beads; a
rusty penknife; a chipped china cat; a birthday card;
a piece of ribbon—all worthless, except to me. They were
my only possessions, which had accompanied me for
so long that they had become part of myself. I could
have left the bag in any of my drawers and no one would
have disturbed it, but I was still young enough to enjoy

a secret hiding place, and this I determined to find for it.

I looked round the room carefully, and then turned my attention to the boxed-in wooden seat set into the window alcove where I sat. I lifted the cushion and found underneath it a lid; and when I opened this, there was a locker that might have been used for toys or shoes, and I noticed the smell again. I popped my bag inside the locker, shut down the lid, and replaced the cushion. It would do for a temporary hidey-hole at least. Then I went downstairs to find Aunt Liss.

She was in the garden, and I asked her for a plot of ground so that I could make a garden of my own. For the first time in my life, I was free to come and go as I pleased, to do as I liked. All about me was the English spring—the tender young green of the trees, lambs in the fields, the sunny tearful days and sharp starry nights of April. I wandered where my fancy led, up onto the moors with my hair blowing wild and the air full of exciting scents and sounds, or down the steep wooded beds of the streams which chattered and gurgled their way to the sea. There I found my first primroses, starring the green banks under the gray-haired ash trees, and near the water, growing in military order, regiments of the slender black-ringed green spikes of mares'-tails. I brought several back with me and stuck them in a jam-jar in the kitchen window, where I kept them till each ring had sprouted lacy fronds of green, wiry as horse hair.

One would have thought my stage was set for certain happiness, but this was not so. I was lonely. I had always lived in a community, in the camps and at the orphanage.

Now I missed the other children, especially Anya who was my friend. Also I was aware of a strangeness, an awkwardness—I did not belong to the secure sheltered world of Aunt Liss on the one hand, and on the other, I had left the rough haphazard ways of my early life behind me. My experience of the camps and in the orphanage had set me apart from ordinary people; I felt marooned on a kind of island of isolation and could not find the bridge. I was angry that I did not fit easily into my new life at the Old Court. Too often I felt restless, dissatisfied with everything, and above all with myself.

Sometimes, I walked home with Rees in the evening, when he had finished his work, to his cottage on the moor, where he lived all alone. Everything was as neat and orderly as any woman could have kept it; and while he made us a cup of tea, he told me about his mother and the maimed wild creatures she had as pets, and the way she tamed the seals. I wished I could have known her. One day, he took me to a little rocky inlet, called Seal Cove; but although we waited for a long time, we saw no seals.

"This is the place where Miss Liss met with her accident," he said. "She fell from the top of the cliff up there, down into the black water, and I pulled her out of the sea on to that ledge below us. It was a terrible day for us all," he muttered, shaking his head. "Terrible." I made a mental note that I must approach this place with the greatest care. As we crossed the fields towards home again, I marveled at Rees's alertness; he missed nothing from the hawk balancing on the wind to the field mouse hiding under a tuft on the path, yet he was as bent as the letter C.

Occasionally in the afternoons people came to tea with Aunt Liss: the vicar and his wife, the doctor, or various old friends who lived near. Aunt Liss liked me to change from my jeans into a frock or skirt on these occasions, and help pass round the lovely cakes and biscuits that Emmy Lee made. Sometimes we had tea in the garden near the old tree that grew by the house, sometimes in the drawing room with its polished floor.

I dreaded those tea parties, for I did not feel at ease with those people. I was sure they despised me for being foreign, and I thought them only half alive. But for Aunt Liss's sake I buttoned in my rebelliousness and behaved properly. It was a great strain.

One evening, after the guests had gone, we sat together in this room and Aunt Liss turned on the radio. They were playing Chopin, which I loved.

When it was finished, Aunt Liss turned to me. "Don't you want to dance to it?" she asked.

I shook my head. The music did not have this effect on me.

"How strange you have not inherited your mother's love of dancing," she went on. "Dancing was so vital to her, so much a part of her, it was as natural to her as breathing. I believe if she had not married your father so young, she might have become a great ballerina. But I needn't tell you all this, you must know more about it than I do. You must have seen her yourself."

I stared at her aghast. My mother . . . dancing? How

could she! And before I could stop myself a great sob tore my throat, and in a paroxysm of anguish I blurted out something I had never meant to say.

"I never saw my mother dance. She could not dance. She could barely hobble. The Nazis tortured her. They burned the soles of her feet."

Aunt Liss's face went ashen, and she put up her hands and covered her eyes, as if shutting out a picture of insupportable horror.

I felt an abyss open between her and me, and I turned and fled from the room, overwhelmed at the cruel shock I had given her. I had not meant to say it, for I knew she could not have known. Though I had understood something before of what my mother had meant when she said she had changed too much to go home to England, I now understood her feelings even better. She had wanted to spare Aunt Liss this horror; she had not meant her ever to know.

I was much too upset myself at the time to try to comfort Aunt Liss. Nor could I have found the right words. I escaped quickly to my room. There I threw myself on my bed and gave way to tears of desolation. But the unsympathetic aloofness of the room had a helpful effect on me, and soon I was able to pull myself together. I washed my face and brushed my hair and went down to the kitchen to help Emmy Lee with the supper.

Nothing more was said at the time by Aunt Liss or by me; but when it was bedtime that evening, I kissed her good night with more tenderness than usual, and she touched my cheek with her hand. "There are things you must try to forget, Nina," she said, gently, and I was grateful to her for asking no questions till I was ready to tell her.

From then, as our relationship developed, there was almost a reversal of our roles; for it was quite apparent to both of us that of the two I was the stronger, the tougher, and Aunt Liss the one in need of protection. Her life had been a sheltered one, while mine had been hard, at times unendurable. I could take whatever might come.

# CHAPTER FIVE

THE SPRING DAYS BLOSSOMED INTO SUMMER, AND AUNT Liss began to agitate about my schooling. Should it be boarding school, or day school in the nearby town? When she asked my opinion, I chose day school without hesitation, for in spite of feeling lonely at the Old Court, I dreaded uprooting myself yet again, and I hoped I might make school friends in the district.

So she arranged that I should start in the autumn term at the high school six miles away. A list of books was sent that I would be expected to have read by then.

My favorite seat for reading was one of the branches of the old weeping ash, and part of every fine day I spent up there with my book.

Growing round the foot of the tree were great clumps
of a strange looking gray-green plant. Rees called it
"Santolina."

Its weird antlered sprigs of foliage I thought intriguing and beautiful, but the scent of its garish yellow
flower, which rose to my perch in the tree, was horrible.
It was a pungent evil smell that I found obnoxious, yet
faintly familiar.

It was several days before I recognized it as the same
unpleasant smell that sometimes hung about my room
. . . Santolina. I wondered how it got there? The windows of my bedroom were on the opposite side of the
house from the old tree, and the flower grew nowhere
else in the garden.

I took the trouble to look the plant up in an old book
of herbs in the library.

"Santolina or Lavender Cotton," I read, "resisteth
poison and helpeth the bitings of venomous beasts. It is
under the dominion of Mercury."

So it was an ancient herb with healing properties.
Why then did it have such an evil smell?

It was all most puzzling and added yet one more mystery to the peculiarities of my bedroom.

On the cliffs one morning, I found a very beautiful
stone, a fossil of smooth polished blue, imprinted with a
shell. I carried it home in my hand to show Aunt Liss;
and after she and Emmy had seen it, I decided to put it
into my relics bag along with my other treasures.

I ran lightly upstairs and paused a moment outside the

door of my room, then burst in suddenly. I always did
this, hoping to catch unawares that hostile presence I
knew was there. But nothing was visible, the room was
aloof and quiet, with sunlight streaming in through the
open windows.

I crossed to the locker in the alcove where my bag
was hidden and dragged off the cushion seat. I opened
the lid and, kneeling down, I put my hand inside to
pull out the bag. At that moment a bird called from
the hill with a note of such piercing sweetness—a curlew
Rees said it was—that I raised my head to listen, leaning
my hand on the floor inside the locker. The board I
leaned on was loose, and my hand pressed one end down
into a cavity below, and brought the other end up like a
seesaw.

I twisted round, the curlew forgotten, and I pressed
the board up and down once or twice. Then I found
that I could lift it right out. Underneath it was a cob-
webby dark hole and I put my hand in gingerly and
felt all round it. At once I touched something hard; a
box of some kind.

My exploring fingers felt along its edge to gauge its
size; then putting both hands into the hole, I carefully
levered it out and lifted it onto the floor.

It was a cardboard shoe box and was covered with
dust and cobwebs, as if it had lain undisturbed for a long
time. Whose secret had I discovered?

My hands trembled with excitement as I lifted off the
lid, and the musty scent of Santolina rose to my nostrils.
I gasped in astonishment at what lay revealed before me.

Bedded down and packed round with the withered foliage and flowers of the herb, lay a beautifully dressed doll. She had a smooth wooden face and her expression was mysterious and sly and knowledgeable, as if she had known all the answers from the beginning of time.

I lifted her out of the box and smoothed with my fingers the satin of her jade-green frock. I turned up the hem to admire her lacy underclothes, all most beautifully hand sewn. Then I began to undress her, untying and unbuttoning garment after garment till she lay naked before me. Her polished wooden body was satin-smooth, her limbs were attached to it with iron pins, her head carved with short wavy hair, and down her spine, cut into the wood were the letters D I D O.

I rubbed my fingers down them. "D I D O. It must be her name," I said aloud.

I held her in my hands for a long time, observing her closely, in detail. She looked ageless, and I felt sure she must be more than a hundred years old, perhaps much more. I wondered what her history had been? Where had she come from? To whom had she belonged? I found her disturbing, a little frightening and . . . wicked!

There was something else I felt about her. She was alien to this ordered and dignified old house, a misfit. She was like a flaming wild poppy in a well-tended rose garden; she was a renegade, she did not belong here. Neither did I. This made a bond, a feeling of kinship between us that attracted me to her immediately.

I wondered if I ought to tell Aunt Liss or Emmy Lee of my discovery. "But why should I? I found her so she is mine, my secret," I said. I began to put her clothes on again, gloating a little over her. I would tell no one nor share her; Dido would be *mine!*

I wrapped her in a clean duster and turned my attention to the box. When I shook the withered Santolina onto a newspaper, I found underneath it in the bottom of the box, half a dozen candle ends and a folded piece of paper. I opened it and read the faintly penciled words.

"Draw a circle counter-clockwise. Set within it salt, a healing herb (Lavender Cotton will do) and fire. Light a candle in the room."

I gave a little gasp of apprehension and my scalp prickled with excitement as I read the words over again. This was witchcraft: magic—"A circle . . . salt . . . fire . . . a healing herb . . ." Lavender Cotton was Santolina. I remembered looking it up and finding that it had medicinal properties. Why a healing plant? Was it perhaps a protection against evil? And fire . . . all those candle ends. I knew about witches. There had been a witch called Olga in one of the camps my mother and I had lived in.

I picked Dido up again and studied her with renewed interest. Was she a witch-doll? Who in this room had dabbled in witchcraft? Who had written out these instructions in magic? Certainly not Aunt Liss; nor my mother. Who then?

"Why, Judith!" I said aloud. "It must have been Judith."

Thoughtfully I laid Dido back in her box and shut down the lid. Then I hid it again under the loose board in the floor of the window seat and put everything back as it was before.

I found that I was trembling with excitement and fear. I sensed that Dido was wicked, dangerous perhaps. I knew that I ought to hand her over to Emmy Lee to destroy; but the temptation to keep her a guilty secret was too great for me.

"I'll be careful," I promised myself. "I'll only play with her occasionally. I'll keep her just for a little while."

I felt sure of my own strength, then.

I was thinking deeply about Dido as I began to go slowly downstairs, intending to make for the kitchen where Emmy Lee was baking Welsh cakes and had offered to teach me to make them, but as I passed Aunt Liss's door she called me. I paid no attention, pretending not to hear, and my feet went steadily on towards the kitchen, against my will almost as if they were under some external control. But when I reached the kitchen door I stopped and forced myself to turn back again to see what Aunt Liss wanted. I was ashamed of myself, and to atone for my strange behavior, I stayed with her for some time, deliberately depriving myself of my cooking lesson with Emmy Lee.

# *CHAPTER SIX*

Aunt Liss had promised, when I left the orphanage, to invite Anya to come to stay with us. Ever since then I had been waiting and longing for her to mention it again, but had not quite liked to remind her. However one morning, about a week after I found Dido, I was in my plot in the garden when the postman arrived on his bicycle. I took the letters from him and ran with them to Aunt Liss.

She looked through them and opened one quickly.

"I'm afraid this will be a great disappointment to you, darling," she said as she read it. "This is from your house mother at the orphanage. Anya has measles and will not be able to come for a week or two. I had written to invite her to stay with us. I meant it to be a surprise for you; I'm so sorry."

"Oh, poor Anya," I said. "Will she be able to come when she's better?"

"I'll arrange her visit as soon as she's recovered," said Aunt Liss. "If you'd like to write to her, I'll enclose the letter in mine."

"Oh, yes," I cried, "I'll do it right now!"

I ran up to my room, trying to hide my disappointment, sat down in the window seat with my writing pad, and began my letter.

But the faint scent of Santolina, which lingered in the room, reminded me of Dido, and I imagined she was knocking on the locker, clamoring to get out. So I threw down my writing and opened the lid of the window seat; I removed the floor board and lifted out the cardboard box. When I opened it, I was struck once again by the extraordinary fascination of the doll. She was really quite beautiful. I took her out of the box, shook out her clothes, and propped her up on the cushioned seat beside me. Her expression was slightly petulant, as if she was annoyed with me. Perhaps she resented being shut up in the box again once I had discovered her, and the shiver of her displeasure chilled me in spite of the sunshine that flooded the room.

I took up my pen and went on with my letter to Anya, but I was uncomfortable and selfconscious under the doll's disapproving scrutiny; my confidence was shaken, my line of contact with Anya was broken. I felt I did not know her any more. It was as if a shadow had come between us.

After a few minutes I gave up and crossed to the window that looked out onto the hills beyond Rees Owen's cottage. I knelt there in the sunshine, taking deep breaths of the thyme-scented air from the moors and the fresh beauty of the morning. Suddenly, piercingly, a curlew called from the hill, breaking the spell of silence. Its wild magical note released the tension in me, and gave me a wonderful feeling of strength and lightness, of escape from the dark power of Dido that shadowed the room behind me.

I jumped up immediately and seized the doll. I stripped off her beautiful clothes, which I tossed into the box, and threw her face downwards on top of them. I shut the lid firmly and put the box back into its hiding place again, and I felt a lot better.

I took up my letter to Anya, meaning to finish it, but the sentences I had written while Dido sat beside me claiming my attention, gave me a horrible shock.

"It will be wonderful to see you again," I had written, "and to have you here with me. I am lonely and bored and although everyone is kind to me they are *too* kind, *too* good, and they are not my sort of people. I am too tough for this tidy sheltered life. It stifles me so that I cannot breathe. I feel I am a stranger, a misfit, I don't belong here, and it makes me restless and *wicked*."

I gulped with shame. *I* had written this about Aunt Liss and Emmy Lee, the people I loved, about the Old Court, my home. I could not believe I had written such horrible things, and yet there they were before my eyes. What on earth had come over me?

I was shocked and frightened, and I tore the letter into small pieces—it was written in Polish to Anya, of course —and I ran downstairs and dropped the pieces into the kitchen stove. Then I went out to the garden and sat down close beside Aunt Liss, close enough to lean my shoulder against her knee, and there I wrote a short note to Anya, saying how much I longed to see her and what a wonderful time we would have together. "You'll like them all," I wrote, "Aunt Liss and Emmy Lee, and Rees, they are the best kind of people."

After that I felt better, and I gave the letter to Aunt Liss to put into hers. A little later I went off to look for Rees, who had promised to find a hedgehog for me to have as a pet.

I knew he was ditching in the field beyond the garden, and as I walked slowly along the path I began to think again about Dido.

From the first moment I had discovered her, I had known that she was wicked, that by keeping her I was playing with fire, with danger. But this was the very thing that fascinated me, that added a secret spice and excitement to my life.

I had thought myself strong enough to resist her power, to keep her under my control. But now I began to realize the influence she could have over me, and I felt helpless before her. As long as she remained in my room, I knew she would compel me oftener and oftener to bring her out of her box, to fondle her and play with her, to dress her up and to admire her smooth exotic face.

What might she demand of me next?

I was frightened of her power over me, but I could not give her up, not just yet.

"But I'll banish her from my room," I promised myself aloud. "I'll find a new hiding place for her today."

Soon I came on Rees trimming the hedge above his newly cleaned ditch. I hurried towards him, calling eagerly, "Rees, Rees. Have you found one? A hedgehog, I mean?"

He turned slowly towards me, his charming smile illuminating his rather grim face. "Here you are," he said, and he put his hand into his deep pocket and pulled out a small hedgehog curled up in a tight ball. I took it from him gingerly, afraid of its prickles, but it did not hurt me.

"Oh, thank you, Rees," I cried. "Isn't he a darling? What shall I give him to eat?"

"He'll find his own food," said Rees. "Slugs, beetles and the like, but you can give him some milk in a saucer; he'll enjoy that."

"But I'll lose him if I let him loose in the garden," I said.

"Bed him down in a box with plenty of leaves," said Rees, "and keep his saucer of milk full. He'll not wander far from it."

I took him back to the house and begged for a box from Emmy Lee, and a saucer of milk. I carried them into the garden and put them under an apple tree. I placed the hedgehog near the milk, and he soon unrolled himself. His black snout pushed over the edge of the saucer into the milk. I put plenty of dry leaves in the box, which I placed on its side, and when he had drunk enough milk, I put him into his bed. Then I ran indoors and went upstairs to my room.

I strode to the window locker and lifted out Dido's box. Without opening it to look at her, I carried it down the stairs and along the passage past the kitchen to the oldest part of the house. Up the wooden steps I went to the attic loft. It was dark up there and unfriendly. I dared not stop or hesitate over what I had to do. If I lifted the lid and looked once more at Dido's face, I knew I would have to take her back with me to my room again. So I opened the nearest black tin trunk and thrust Dido's box into it. I slammed it shut and fled down the steps and out into the yard.

My heart beat loudly, and I felt as guilty as if I had done some fearful thing. Just then the lunch bell rang, and the savory smell of Emmy Lee's cooking coming from the kitchen door, made me forget everything, except that I was ravenously hungry.

# CHAPTER SEVEN

I WENT OFF TO BED RATHER EARLY THAT NIGHT. AUNT Liss had been teaching me to play chess, but I was restless and edgy and had found it hard to concentrate.

I read for a little while after I got into bed, but when I turned off the light, I could not sleep.

Moonlight flooded the room with an eeriness that made me more wide awake than ever. I tossed and turned, throwing off my bedclothes then pulling them on again; listening to the striking of the slow hours on the grandmother clock in the hall; starting from a doze at the call of the hunting owl. I tried to soothe my mind by making plans of what Anya and I would do when she came to stay; I thought of the little hedgehog in its box under the apple tree; of Emmy Lee making delicious pies in her friendly kitchen; of Aunt Liss reading aloud to me with Gillie sighing at her feet, warm comforting thoughts.

Still I lay awake thinking of Dido, grieving for her, missing her.

At last I could stand it no longer. I got up, seized my flashlight, and crept down the stairs, making for the old loft above the kitchen.

The house cracked and muttered in its sleep, full of tiny noises that passed unnoticed by day.

When I came to the kitchen where Gillie slept, I paused to whisper to him so that he would know it was me and not rouse the household by barking. I climbed the creaking steps to the hostile blackness of the loft, and taking a deep breath to give me courage, I plunged towards the metal trunk and lifted out Dido's box. Clutching it to me, I hurried down the steps and through the house back to my room again, my heart thumping and my knees weak. When I reached it, I sank thankfully onto my bed and took off the lid of the box. There lay Dido, face downwards on her beautiful clothes, rejected, in disgrace.

I lifted her out and looked at her fearfully. Her expression was venomous, malevolent. I knew she would pay me back for punishing her.

Somehow, I must pacify her, make amends. So I dressed her with care in all her finery and placed her at the open window, hidden by the curtain in case Emmy

Lee should discover her before I woke.

It must have been about four o'clock in the morning and a faint grayness showed that dawn was near. I leaned out over the window sill as the first early birds began to sing, and then with a lift of the heart, I heard the curlew.

I fell into bed and was sound asleep in a moment.

I was wakened by Emmy Lee knocking on the door and in a minute she put her head round it.

"Eight o'clock, Nina," she cried. "You are a sleepy head this morning!"

"Go away," I said sharply. "I'll be down in a minute." I scrambled out of bed, for I did not want her to come further into the room lest she discover Dido.

She closed the door, but not before I had caught the cheerful smell of sizzling bacon.

I felt exhausted from lack of sleep, but relieved that I no longer had to feel guilty about Dido. When I lifted back the curtain and took her in my hands, her expression was almost benign. She was in her gentlest mood. I was forgiven.

"Now listen, Dido," I said aloud to her, "by day you must stay hidden when I am not in the room, for I have a strong feeling that they would not approve of your being here. You must not be found, no one must know about you; but all night long you shall be free. Do you understand?"

Her smile was enigmatic and I could not read her expression, but I thought it held a hint of triumph—Dido had won. I laid her gently back in the box again, twitching the folds of her skirt into place. I left the lid off, and I returned her to her hiding place under the window seat.

Hurriedly I dressed and ran down for breakfast.

When I returned afterwards to make my bed, I screwed a small hook into the wood by the window, behind the curtain, and knotted a piece of ribbon to it. At night when I sat Dido by the open window, I would tie the ribbon round her waist so that she would not slip or be blown down by the wind.

For about a week all seemed well, and I thought I had got the better of her—and then the dreams began.

The first one was more strange than horrible. I dreamed that I felt a queer prickling in my feet and my hands, and when I looked at them, they were not my hands and feet but the furry paws of a black kitten.

I woke in the very early morning with my heart fluttering, anxious and apprehensive; and as I tumbled out of bed and crossed the room to see if Dido was all right, I heard the first curlew calling from the moor. Its magic had broken my bad dream, and I was grateful.

The next dream was worse: I had changed completely into a black kitten, and from the other side of a great patch of low-growing sea holly, Dido stood calling for me to come to her. The prickles of the holly were piercing my feet, but her summons was imperious, insistent, and I dared not disobey. Cautiously, painfully, I made my way towards her, across the torturing prickles, while she urged me mercilessly to come more quickly.

As I approached her, the patch of sea holly grew and

grew, so that I knew I could never reach her, and I also knew she would punish me terribly for failing to obey her command. I was in despair, and the tender pads of my feet hurt intolerably, but still she urged me on.

Then suddenly a curlew called, once, piercingly, and woke me—the nightmare was over.

Anxiously in the gray light of early morning, I felt my hands and feet, examining them carefully—they were my own, and untouched. But I dared not go to sleep again, I was afraid that the horrible dream might be repeated.

I must have looked tired at breakfast time, for both Aunt Liss and Emmy Lee asked what was wrong with me. Was I ill? Had I not slept well? Was I worried about something?

To all their inquiries I answered bluntly, "I'm all right."

I dared not tell them the truth. I felt that somehow Dido would know and punish me, torture me with even worse dreams. I could not risk it.

But I began to feel really frightened and to wonder where it was all going to end.

Dido had to be destroyed—and *I* must do it!

# CHAPTER EIGHT

A FEW MORE DAYS PASSED BEFORE I HAD ANOTHER NIGHT-mare; but when it came it was worse than ever.

Once again I became the black kitten, bullied and tormented by Dido. I was terribly thirsty and Dido offered me a deep saucer of milk, but to reach it I had to walk across the top of a vast hot stove. I started to cross it, but once on it I could not get off, and Dido with the enticing saucer of milk kept changing her position. I burned my paws more and more, and I began to mew and cry with the pain. In desperation I took a great leap towards the window, but instead of reaching it, I landed once more on the hottest part of the stove—and Dido stood and laughed at me.

I woke in agony. So vivid had been the nightmare that I could not believe that my feet were whole and unburned. I sat up in bed and felt them gingerly all over, pinching first the soles and then the heels. They were perfectly sound; it was only a dream after all. I realized that this torment could not, must not, go on, and I began to plan again how to rid myself of Dido.

At least I could punish her at once while my anger with her was strong enough to overcome my fear. I went and pulled her roughly from behind the curtain, and shook her till I had worked off my rage. Then, taking care not to look at her face, I stripped off her clothes and pushed her into her box, which I returned to its usual place.

I felt one of my black moods coming on, a misery of frustration that made me depressed and vindictive. I knew that Aunt Liss and Emmy Lee were puzzled and worried by them, as I was myself, and I felt that it was all Dido's fault. I must do something, and do it quickly.

For once I was ready before Emmy Lee knocked on my door. While I was dressing I had made up my mind what to do with Dido.

I would take her to the highest point of the cliffs and hurl her out to sea, and the waves would carry her away out of my sight forever. Then I would be rid of her. I began to breathe more freely, and I went down to breakfast almost lightheartedly.

Afterwards I visited the hedgehog in its box in the garden. It was safe, contentedly tucked up in its leaves, asleep. I picked it up, along with its empty saucer and carried it to the kitchen. Emmy Lee was not there, so I filled the saucer with milk and took it round the house into the sun. I put the little creature down on the grass and crouched beside it, still as a mouse, waiting for it to uncurl itself and drink. In a moment it did so, and I watched it, enchanted at its trust in me.

Then through the open window beyond me, I heard Aunt Liss's voice; she was talking to Emmy Lee. It was me they were discussing, and I knew I ought to make my presence known or go away at once; but I didn't, I stayed where I was to listen, an inquisitive eavesdropper.

"She has changed, Emmy," said Aunt Liss. "There must be something wrong. She is so easily upset, so unpredictable and secretive. Whatever can be the matter? She seemed happy when she first came."

"Maybe she is more disappointed than we know that her friend can't come and is feeling a bit lonely," said Emmy Lee comfortingly. "I must say she looks tired and nervy, as if she doesn't sleep well. Do you think a tonic would help her? Of course she's just at the growing stage, starting her teens and all that, probably that's the trouble."

"I hope you're right," Aunt Liss replied. "I wish I could think so, but I'm afraid it is something more serious than that, something frightening her. Emmy . . . I'm afraid she might have found that horrible doll . . . that she has fallen under Dido's spell, as Judith did."

"Oh, nonsense, Miss Liss, don't distress yourself by imagining such things," said Emmy. "Nina will get over this moodiness. I'll bring her a tonic from the chemist when I go into Newcove tomorrow. We must just be patient with her. She's at a difficult age."

I picked up my hedgehog and crept away unnoticed back to the orchard to puzzle this out. So Aunt Liss and Emmy Lee knew about Dido, knew she was wicked. Judith had fallen under her spell, just as I had. And I had been right about Judith. It was she who had loved and cherished Dido, who had made all those beautiful clothes for her, who had hidden her away so that Aunt Liss and Emmy Lee could not find her. But Judith had been cruel and spiteful; it was she who had tormented my mother's childhood, and I hated her for that.

What if I should become like Judith? What if Dido's power should change me into someone like my grandmother? It was a horrible, terrifying thought. I must rid myself of Dido *now* before it was too late.

I went at once to collect my swimming things and stuffed them into my duffle bag, and I pulled Dido out of her box and thrust her, face downwards, into the bottom of the bag.

I called to Aunt Liss that I was going for a swim.

"Don't go in alone," she cautioned me as I started off down the lane and across the fields towards the cliffs.

I made straight for the highest point, and I took Dido out of the bag. I looked cautiously round; there was no one about. Then, without giving myself a moment of farewell, lest I weaken, I shut my eyes and hurled her with all my strength out to sea.

She fell towards the waves, and I turned and fled

downhill to the little bay that I loved, to wait for the
bathers whom I saw coming from the farm.

I plunged in and swam, mingling with the visitors who
were there on holiday; and when I came out of the sea
I felt wonderful, fresh and tingling with life, as if I had
cast a load off my back into the sparkling water.

On the way home I picked a posy of honeysuckle for
Aunt Liss and sang at the top of my voice as I crossed
the fields.

My room when I reached it felt different, fresh and
clean and—empty. The shadow had lifted, Dido and her
tormenting presence was gone. I had rid myself of her

at last—and yet, perversely, I missed her, and half wished her back again.

The next morning I had to take a message to the farm in the bay, and after I had delivered it, I ran down to the empty beach. It was too early to swim, and there was no one about. I hopped from side to side across the fringe of seaweed left by the tide, and as I glanced along it my body froze into stillness—there on the seaweed, washed up and left by the tide, there indestructible, invincible, lay Dido.

With a cry I picked her up and looked into her face. Reproach I saw there, and mockery and triumph, and I hated her for it.

Once again she had won! However could I have forgotten she was made of wood, and wood floats. I felt I would never get rid of her now, and my heart sank with despair as I thought of the renewed nightmares, the terror of her wicked power over me. I knew how she would torture and revenge herself on me. And yet in spite of all, I was still fond of her. I was glad to have her back again, even only as my safety valve, my scapegoat. For sometimes, when for no apparent reason a rage blew up in me, I was able to work off my bad temper on Dido. By bashing her smooth face on the cushions of the window seat till my arms ached, I was able at last to calm myself again without anyone knowing —but only when I was too angry to be afraid of her. Without a word, I tucked her inside my jersey and carried her home.

# CHAPTER NINE

Dido was reinstated and dressed again in all her finery. By night she sat at my window; by day while I was out of the room, she lay in her box like a sleeping beauty. I found myself spending more and more time with her, talking to her, flattering her, cajoling her, seeking to please her. I even began to draw sketches of her and was surprised to find how natural and easy it was. I drew other things as well, and I was pleased with the results and determined to learn as much as I could when I got to school, to work really hard and perhaps become an artist.

The bottle of tonic that Emmy Lee had bought for

me was swallowed three times a day under protest. I can't say that it made me feel any different, only hungrier. The weather for a week or two played into my hands, with driving rain and gales, which kept me mainly indoors, and I was able to spend a great deal of time in my room, leading a secret hidden life of my own, with Dido.

"Whatever do you do all alone up there?" asked Aunt Liss. "I see so little of you now, Nina."

"Oh, I read, and think, and draw," I replied shortly.

"Draw? What do you draw?" asked Aunt Liss, almost suspiciously.

"Oh, birds and the old tree in the garden, things I can see from my window, sometimes people, Rees." I was not going to give anything away.

She looked relieved and tranquil again.

"Do let me see your sketches sometime, darling," she begged. "You may have talent. Both your grandmother and your grandfather were artists, you know."

I carefully separated the drawings of Dido from the others I had done, and the next day I brought the rest down to show to her.

She encouraged me very much and thought my sketches most promising.

"I will speak to your art teacher when you go to school," said Aunt Liss. "You must have every chance to develop your talent. These drawings are good."

For a day or two I felt happier, and then the bad dreams started again, as I knew they would, and they were worse than ever—much worse.

No sooner had I fallen asleep than I changed into the black kitten, but now Dido mounted on my back, rode me all night long across the fields and up onto the wild heathery hills, past the row of besoms kept for fire-beaters, like broomsticks waiting for witches. She drove me on, faster and faster, so that I woke in the morning utterly exhausted. Worse still, sometimes she nearly frightened me to death.

Once, in bright moonlight she galloped me towards a hedge of hawthorn. Out of its thicket I saw two snakes rearing and swaying in the air, towards and away from each other.

"Jump the hedge and pass between them," hissed Dido in my ear. "If you miss, they'll strike you dead."

Half dead already from fright, I gathered myself for a tremendous leap. As I passed between them, I saw that the snakes were nothing but two tall evening primroses harmlessly swaying in the wind. Dido shrieked with mocking laughter at my distress.

Another night I carried her over the stubble fields, racing the setting moon in my headlong flight. Suddenly great wings shadowed me, and high above I saw a huge bird of prey poised on the wind. I felt myself shrink to mouse size, and Dido leaped off my back, abandoning me as I waited, helpless, for the grip of those cruel talons. Her mocking laughter pursued me from the shadows, while I searched in vain for cover.

Always the early curlew calling from the moor broke my dream and ended my terror. Its magic woke me to safety, to sanity.

The worse the nightmare, the harder I tried to pacify Dido by giving her more of my attention. I even turned my pet hedgehog loose to roam away from the garden. I thought that Dido might be jealous of him for the time I spent with him.

After dinner one evening Aunt Liss brought out of her desk a small leather jewel case. She unlocked it and showed me her collection of antique brooches. They were mostly large and I thought rather clumsy, but one of them caught my eye because of its marvelous color.

"That is a ruby," Aunt Liss explained. "Your taste is good, Nina. You have picked out the most valuable brooch of them all."

She put it into my hand and I held it, turning it about so that it caught the light and blazed with crimson fire.

"It is a marvelous color. I've never seen anything like it," I cried, and Aunt Liss pinned it onto my dress and let me wear it till bed time. I watched her put it away with the others into the case, which she locked and put back into the desk.

I took as long as I could getting ready for bed that night. I dreaded going to sleep because of what I might dream. When at last I was ready, I pocketed my pride and crept down to the kitchen to beg Emmy Lee for a candle.

"Whatever next?" cried Emmy. "What do you want with a candle?"

She looked at me almost suspiciously, and I caught my breath as I remembered the old candle ends in Dido's box.

"It won't flicker or blow out will it?" I asked anxiously.

Immediately Emmy's face softened and she looked at me with concern.

"It's the dark is it?" she said. "Are you having bad dreams, dearie? Would you like to come down to your mother's room, or in beside me?"

I shook my head. "I'll be all right with a candle," I snapped. And Emmy went to the cupboard to find one.

"You come down to me if you waken in the night," she said kindly as I bade her good-night. She hugged me warmly and would have come upstairs to tuck me in, but I would not let her in case she discovered Dido on her perch by the window.

Before I got into bed, I lit the candle and put it on the table beside me. I hoped it might keep me awake for a while. At least its tiny flame was comforting, a sort of protection from the terror that lurked in my room ready to submerge me as soon as I slept.

My dreams that night took a different form. I was myself, I kept my own shape.

I dreamed that Dido was threatening me, urging me to do something for her; something wrong, something wicked that revolted me so much that my whole being protested against it. It was something connected with Aunt Liss whom Dido hated. At last it became clear to me what she was trying to make me do. I was to get the ruby brooch for her, the brooch from Aunt Liss's collection. Dido wanted it. Dido must have it, and I must get it for her.

"But that would be stealing!" I cried. "Stealing from Aunt Liss. No, no! I cannot. I will not do it!"

Then Dido began to torment me, to pinch me and pull my hair, to scream threats at me. Still I refused to do what she wanted, although her shrill rage nearly drove me mad.

Suddenly in my dream her tactics changed and she became gentle and persuasive, and I thought I had won till she said in a smooth and deadly voice, "You had better do what I tell you. If you don't an accident might happen—to your precious Aunt Liss. She could slip on the stairs, or trip over something, it could easily happen, you know, easily."

Then panic took hold of me and I was convinced that unless I did as she told me, Dido would carry out her threat to harm Aunt Liss.

"Get me the brooch, Nina. Think how beautiful the ruby will look on the green of my dress," Dido's coaxing voice persisted. "Just let me wear it once, only for one night, please," she pleaded.

Her wheedling voice trailed on. I was in despair. What was I to do?

I woke from my dream suddenly, with a terrible feeling of guilt and shame. I found myself standing by Aunt Liss's desk in her sitting room. My bare feet were icy cold. The drawer of the desk stood open, and from the cushion of the leather jewel case in my hand, the ruby brooch glowed and shone in the candlelight. What on earth was I doing here?

Like a flash I remembered my dream and what I had

come to do at Dido's command. The shock was so great
that my legs gave way and I sat down trembling in
Aunt Liss's chair. My teeth began to chatter as I realized
the extent of Dido's power over me, and the dreadful
thing I had nearly done for her. What else might she
compel me to do in my sleep?

This time I had wakened before the damage was done.
Next time I might not be so lucky.

I did not entirely believe that Dido was able to harm
Aunt Liss as she had threatened to do, but I dared not
take the risk. No harm would ever come to Aunt Liss if
I could help it.

At that moment I began to realize how much Aunt
Liss meant to me. I loved her more than anyone else
in the world.

*Dido must go.*

This time there would be no mistake, no reprieve.
This time I would not fail. By threatening to harm Aunt
Liss, Dido had ordered her own destruction.

I returned the jewel case to its place, shut the drawer
and locked it, but I did not dare go back to my bedroom that night. So I felt my way, by the tiny light of
my candle, up the stairs and along the passage to Emmy
Lee's room. I crept in at her door and whispered shakily,
"Emmy, Emmy, it's me."

"Come in my dearie, come in," said Emmy Lee, and
she moved over in her warm bed to make room for me.

# CHAPTER TEN

WHEN EMMY ROSE AT SIX O'CLOCK AS WAS HER CUSTOM, I too got up.

It was a shining morning, clear and serene, without a puff of wind.

"I'm going down to the beach," I told Emmy, "but not to bathe. No one will be there yet. I'll be back for breakfast."

I went purposefully up to my room to dress, my decision to destroy Dido unshaken, although the terrors of the night had faded.

My room waited for me lit by sunbeams, but hostile, ominous.

The horrid smell of Santolina polluted the air. It seemed to concentrate around Dido where she sat in judgment, a witch doll, waiting for me.

I turned my back on her and pulled on my clothes. Then resolutely I crossed the room to the window and seized her.

Turning her face from me, I undressed her and pushed her into her box along with her trappings—everything that belonged to her, everything—there must not be a trace of her left.

I put a box of matches in my pocket and slipped out of the side door of the house with Dido's box under my arm. What I had to do, I must do quickly.

On my way to the beach I picked up all the sticks I could find, and when I reached the bay I collected dead gorse and heather, and pieces of dry driftwood long ago washed up by the tide, and piled it all up on top of a huge flat stone into a great pyre.

I had chosen the beach for safety. Here there was no danger of the fire spreading, for it was isolated on the sand; there was nothing near to catch alight.

When all was ready, I struck a match and the dry gorse caught. In a moment the flames were flickering, then roaring through the sticks. When they were well alight and crackling fiercely, into the heart of the fire I thrust Dido. I piled her beautiful clothes on top of her and tore the box into fragments and threw them on too.

The blaze became hotter as I piled on more wood, and I used a long stick to prevent any pieces from falling off.

The fierce flames leaped and roared, and I worked like a maniac breaking up wood and piling it on, poking the embers round the edge into the middle again, driving myself into furious activity to prevent myself from thinking about what I was doing, from having any regrets.

The intense heat drove me back, and with my arm I had to protect my face from burning.

At last it was over. The flames began to die down, the smouldering red embers to cool. There could be nothing left of Dido, Dido whom I had feared and hated and —loved.

I threw myself down on the ground and burst into wild sobs. Never again would I tremble in a sweat of fear on the edge of the kitten nightmare, never again would Dido threaten Aunt Liss or terrify me by her wicked power, and yet my overwhelming feeling was one of desolation, of irreparable loss. Dido was gone forever, and I was left, alone.

Gradually my sobs subsided and I grew quiet. I dried my eyes and got up to finish the job.

I picked up a long stick and approached the bonfire to prod it into final activity, to make quite certain that no trace of the doll was left.

But Dido had one last word for me.

As I bent over the ashes there was a sudden, violent explosion. The great flat stone in the heart of the fire burst into a hundred pieces, and flew at me through the air. They fell on my hair, my face, my clothes, my arms, burning and blistering me, and one piece dropped inside my shirt branding me. I screamed with pain and fright and rushed as I was into the sea to cool my burns, while tears of rage poured down my cheeks.

I hated Dido then, and forever more. She had done her best to set me on fire, to destroy me. This was the end. Her spell was broken. I would never forgive her, never!

After a while when I felt better, I plodded back up the beach and began to dig with a flat stone a deep hole in the sand beside the bonfire.

I scooped the ashes and charred fragments into it, filled it up with sand, and made it all clean and smooth and new again.

"Hullo!" said a voice behind me, and I turned to find a boy of about sixteen, looking on with interest at what I was doing.

"I am David Lewis," he said smiling. "That's our farm," nodding towards the house beyond the beach. "I just got home last night from school. You must be Miss Liss's niece, Nina Grenville?"

"Oh, my name . . ." I had been about to contradict him, to tell him my name was Nina Rolska or Kostarska, but something stopped me, a craving to belong, to have roots, the Grenville roots of my grandfather, and I found myself nodding and accepting what he had said.

"Yes, yes," I answered, simply. "I am Nina Grenville."

"Have you been burying treasure or something?" David continued, pointing towards the newly smoothed sand and the stone in my hand. "And what have you done to your face?"

"It was the bonfire; I got burned," I answered. Then, surprising myself, I added, "I have been burying my past."

"That's right!" said David approvingly, as if it were the most natural thing to be doing. "You're one of us now, you know. Well, I must be getting back to help my father, but I'll be seeing you."

He lifted his hand in greeting and, turning, strode off toward the farm, leaving me dazed and happy.

"Nina Grenville. You're one of us now."

I repeated his words slowly, savoring their full meaning, and with mounting joy I discovered that they were true.

Suddenly, incredibly, I had clicked into place. I was not a stranger any more—I belonged. I was Nina Melissa Grenville of the Old Court.

I rose to my feet and ran for home, across the summer fields to breakfast.

When I reached the garden, Rees was already at work there.

"Your hedgehog is back," he said, giving me his sidelong glance. "Rolled up in his box, snug as you please. He must have missed you; you see, he's come home!"

A surge of delight, warming and comforting, rose up in me at his words. I was not friendless after all.

I hurried into the kitchen and Emmy Lee's stocky figure, bending over the sizzling pan of bacon and eggs, sent such a warmth of love pulsing through me that I ran across to her and gave her a tremendous hug.

"What's happened to you?" she cried. "You're hurt, your face and your arms and legs, and you're dripping wet!"

Then as she looked at me more closely her anxious expression changed.

"But you're better, dearie," she said. "You look different, as if you'd shed a load. Everything's going to be all right now, and you'll settle down here with us. Come till I see to those sore places, what happened?"

"Emmy," I said. "Emmy, I've burned Dido—burned her up, destroyed her forever!"

Emmy stared at me as if she had seen a ghost.

"Burned Dido?" she repeated. "Whatever do you mean?"

So I told her the whole story from the time I found the doll. "I had to destroy her, and I had to do it myself," I explained. "And now I think it was a debt I owed to the Old Court. I had to earn my place here, to earn the right to call this my home and I've done it by ridding the house of its curse, of Dido. She nearly got me in the end." I laughed ruefully, feeling round one of the burns.

Emmy who had even let the toast scorch while she listened to me, snatched a tube of ointment from the drawer in the kitchen table and began to squeeze it onto my hurts. Her face was grim, her mouth pursed as it always was when she was angry.

"I'm s-sorry," I faltered. "Dido didn't belong to me. Perhaps I should not have done it?"

Emmy turned on me, her eyes blazing.

"You did right!" she cried. "That doll was evil! If I could have laid hands on her, she'd have been destroyed long ago. The trouble she has caused. And that you should find her, and fall under her spell—it's too much!"

"But Emmy, it's finished," I pointed out. "Dido's gone, and somehow she has helped me to settle into my place here."

Emmy nodded, although she was still frowning.

"Yes, she's gone, thank God," she said. "Dido has been the curse of this house for far too long."

"But she didn't have any power over Aunt Liss, or my mother or you!" I exclaimed. "Only over my grandmother and me. Why was that?"

"Because you were the two who loved her, and we are influenced by those we love," said Emmy.

I looked at her apprehensively as a thought struck me.

"Judith was wicked. She was cruel to my mother," I said slowly. "I loved Dido, too. Am I wicked like my grandmother?"

"No, of course not," said Emmy emphatically. "You were confused and lonely and you lost your way a little. Now you have found it again."

I nodded. I knew Emmy was wise, and what she said was true. I went on thinking for a little, trying to find an explanation for it all.

"I might have become like my grandmother Judith," I muttered, and I shuddered to think of the dark secrets she had practiced in my room with Dido.

"You needn't worry about that now," said Emmy comfortingly. "You'll grow up to be like Miss Liss and your mother."

"Oh, I'm glad I destroyed Dido!" I exclaimed. "It was a hard thing to do when I loved her so much."

"You love Miss Liss more, much more," said Emmy. "That's why you were able to get rid of Dido. We'll keep all this to ourselves, you and me; there's no need to distress Miss Liss with it, unless she asks me about Dido again. Then I'll have to tell her. Now come and I'll help you change your clothes and clean up, dearie, before you have your breakfast."

Aunt Liss had already poured out her coffee, as I slipped into the morning room, apologizing for being late, and bent over her chair to kiss her good morning.

"Whatever have you been doing to yourself?" she asked noticing my burned places.

"I made a bonfire on the beach and a hot stone blew up and hit me," I said. "It's nothing."

Aunt Liss smiled and shook her head at me. Then she picked up a telegram that lay on her plate.

"This is from the orphanage," she said. "Anya is better and will be coming to stay with us at the end of the week. Would you like to share your room with her?"

"Oh yes, oh thank you!" I cried impulsively. "Oh, dear Aunt Liss, how good you are to me. I want to stay here with you forever and ever."

I felt too excited to eat much breakfast. As soon as we had finished and I had helped Emmy to clear away, I filled a saucer with milk for my hedgehog and hurried with it into the garden. He was still fast asleep, rolled up in his box, so I did not disturb him but left his milk beside him.

Great curtains of honeysuckle trailed their sweetness along the hedges, and I picked a huge bunch of it and arranged it in a bowl. I carried it up to my room and set it on the window ledge.

Then I stood looking round my room, slowly, critically.

It was all sun and light; no trace remained of Dido's threatening shadow which had hung over it for so long. The room was empty and pure. Instead of the evil smell of Santolina, honeysuckle now filled the air with its fresh country sweetness.

I began to plan how to arrange the room for Anya's visit.

A few moments later Emmy Lee called me to help her as she came stumping up to the top floor with her arms full of clean bed linen, pillows and blankets.

"There's a folding bed next door," she said. "We'll fetch it in for your friend in a minute when I get my breath back."

We sat down on my bed together and began to laugh at ourselves, panting and puffing with our exertions.

Emmy looked round the room, nodding her head in approval and sniffing appreciatively.

"It's nice that your friend Anya is coming," she remarked. "She'll be company for you till you go to
school."

And suddenly I felt secure and happy with a happiness I had never expected to know, a gentle glowing
happiness which burned in me with a clear steady flame.

RUTH M. ARTHUR was born in Glasgow, Scotland. She attended schools in Scotland, and then Froebel Training College, Roehampton, near London. After graduation, she taught kindergarten until her marriage.

She and her husband now live in Surrey, England. They are the parents of two sons and four daughters, one of whom is married and lives in the United States. Her interests outside of her family and her writing include the theater and cooking. *Dragon Summer* and *My Daughter, Nicola* are the two books she has written that have been published in the United States.